P.S. good

"I've missed you," Li
dumped me last Mar

"I didn't dump you. How c
weren't together."

"Yeah, we were. From that first night, I wasn't with anyone but you. How about you?"

"No. But you know what I mean. It wasn't serious. We weren't even dating."

"Karin."

"What?"

"Shut up." He stole a quick, perfect kiss. Her lips burned at the brief contact. She yearned—she really did. Every molecule in her body hungered for more.

And he knew it, too.

He knew it and he gave her exactly what she couldn't stop herself from wanting. Lowering his amazing mouth, he settled it more firmly over hers.

* * *

THE BRAVOS OF VALENTINE BAY:
They're finding love—and having babies!—
in the Pacific Northwest

Dear Reader,

Widowed single mom Karin Killigan got married ten years ago because she was pregnant. The marriage ended in tragedy. She's never doing that again.

But then last Christmas, she threw caution to the winds and began a secret affair with an old high school flame, Liam Bravo. Being with Liam was the perfect occasional escape from her busy life as a hardworking single mother of two—or it was until the impossible happened and she ended up accidentally pregnant. Again.

Liam Bravo has always kind of skated on the surface of life. He owns a successful trucking company, has a big house in Astoria, Oregon, and for those important emotional connections, he has a large, loving family of Bravos in beautiful Valentine Bay.

What more could a guy want?

Well, the truth is, he's always carried a bit of a torch for Karin. And when he finds out she's having his baby, he's all in from day one. How many ways can a man show a woman that's he's the one she should marry? Liam Bravo is determined to discover them all. No matter how she tries to resist him, he won't give up trying to get it right, to claim Karin's heart and a place at her side.

I hope you get as much satisfaction as I did watching Liam come into his own as he learns how to love and be a part of something bigger than himself. We all need to remember not to give up until we get it right—especially when it comes to love.

Have a beautiful holiday season, everyone. May your Hanukkah be rich in tradition, your Christmas glorious and your New Year the happiest yet!

Christine

The Right Reason to Marry

Christine Rimmer

Recycling programs
for this product may
not exist in your area.

ISBN-13: 978-1-335-57424-4

The Right Reason to Marry

Copyright © 2019 by Christine Rimmer

Printed in U.S.A.

Christine Rimmer came to her profession the long way around. She tried everything from acting to teaching to telephone sales. Now she's finally found work that suits her perfectly. She insists she never had a problem keeping a job—she was merely gaining "life experience" for her future as a novelist. Christine lives with her family in Oregon. Visit her at christinerimmer.com.

For MSR, always.

Chapter One

It was a cloudy Friday afternoon in mid-October when Karin Killigan finally had to face the unsuspecting father of her unborn child.

It happened at Safeway, of all places. He was going in as she went out.

She had her hands full of plastic shopping bags. Her mind was on dinner and the thousand and one things she needed to whip into shape at the office before the baby came. She was staring straight ahead and didn't even see him.

But Liam Bravo saw *her*.

He grabbed her arm. "Karin. My God."

His touch, coupled with the low, rich sound of his voice, set off a chain reaction of emotional explosions inside her. Shock. Guilt. Total embarrassment. A flare of thoroughly inappropriate desire. She let out a ridiculous squeak of surprise and almost dropped a bag full of dairy products as she blinked down at his hand on her arm. Even through the barrier of her coat and the sweater beneath it, she could feel his heat and his strength.

Slowly, she forced her gaze upward to his gorgeous face. The cool autumn wind stirred his dark blond hair and his sun-kissed brows had drawn together over those summer-sky eyes of his.

Somehow, she made herself speak. "Hello, Liam."

"Excuse me." The impatient voice from directly behind her reminded her sharply that they were blocking both doors.

"Come on." Liam tugged her away from the doors and along a short concrete walkway.

She followed numbly, despising herself for never quite working up the nerve to break the big news to him, thus forcing them both to face it now—at Safeway, of all the impossible places.

"Here." He pulled her in close to the brick wall of the building, between a bin full of pumpkins and stacks of bundled kindling. "Let me help you with those." He made a grab for the shopping bags dangling from both of her hands.

"No." She shook her head at him. "I've got them. I'm fine." Total lie. She was very far from fine.

"You sure?"

"Positive," she said way too brightly. "Thanks. I'm, um, really surprised to see you here." Understatement of the decade. He lived in nearby Astoria and somehow, since the last time she'd seen him the previous March, she'd never once run into him in Valentine Bay. Until now. It wasn't that she'd been avoiding him, exactly. But she certainly hadn't sought him out. "I mean, there's a Safeway in Astoria, right?"

"I stopped in to see Percy and Daffy and this store was on my way home." Percy and Daffodil Valentine were brother and sister. Neither had ever married. In their eighties now, Liam's great-uncle and -aunt lived in an ancient Victorian mansion on the edge of Valentine City Park.

"Oh, I see," she said, because he'd fallen silent and it seemed that she ought to say something.

His gaze had wandered downward to her giant belly, only to quickly jerk back up to her face again. "This is awkward." *Oh, no kidding.* "Please don't be offended..."

"No. Of course not." How could she be? She should have told him months ago, on the night she broke it off with him. But she was a big, fat coward. She hadn't told him then, nor had she managed to work up the courage to call him and ask for a meeting. And now the poor guy had to find out like this. Her cheeks and neck were too hot. They must be flaming red. And her heart? It pounded so hard she couldn't hear herself think.

"You're pregnant," he said.

"How did you guess?" It was a weak joke and neither of them laughed.

Beneath his golden tan, his face seemed to be growing progressively paler. "I'm sorry, but I couldn't help thinking that..." He faltered, which broke her heart a little. Liam Bravo never faltered. He was always so smooth. Even way back in high school, he could make a girl's clothes fall off with just his smile. He wasn't smiling now, though. He drew in a shaky breath. "I have to know. Is it...?"

There really was no putting this off any longer, so she answered the question he couldn't seem to ask. "Yes, Liam. It's your baby."

He flinched and his eyes widened. He started to

reach for her again, caught himself and let his arm drop to his side. After that, he just stood there staring at her, his sexy mouth hanging open.

God. What a horrible way to tell him. But at least she'd finally done it.

People bustled by them, going in and out of the store. "We can't do this here," she said. When he only continued to gape at her, she went on, "Tell you what. I'm going straight home…"

A low sound escaped him, kind of a cross between a grunt and sigh, but no actual words came out.

"Home," she repeated. "The house on Sweetheart Cove? I'll be there the rest of the day. Feel free to drop by when you're ready to talk." Carefully, so as not to bump him with her bags of groceries, she turned and made for her car.

He didn't say anything or try to stop her. But she knew that wouldn't last. He was bound to have questions—a million of them. Starting with *why the hell didn't you tell me*? She figured she had an hour, tops, before he appeared at her door.

Probably breaking the land speed record for a hugely pregnant woman on foot, she waddled toward the relative safety of her Chevy Traverse.

Karin lived with her dad, Otto Larson, and her two children, Ben and Coco, on the first floor of a large beach house owned by her brother, Sten. As she pulled the Traverse into the garage beneath the house, her dad came down the inside stairs, seven-year-old Coco close on his heels.

Otto went straight to the hatch in back to get the groceries.

Coco, in blue tights, red shorts, a blue T-shirt and

shiny red rain boots, had stopped at the foot of the stairs to spin in a circle. The kid-size red blanket tied around her neck for a cape fluttered as she twirled. "Mommy, I'm Supergirl!" she shouted as Karin carefully lowered herself from behind the wheel. "Don't worry, I will save you! I have *vast* superhuman strength, speed and *stanima*, X-ray vision, super breath and also, I can fly." Arms out, she "flew" at Karin, who laughed in spite of what had just gone down at Safeway.

Coco halted at Karin's big belly. Reaching out her small arms and tipping her head back, she gave both Karin and the unborn baby inside her a hug. "I love you, Mommy, and I love our baby, too!" Coco beamed a smile so big it showed the gap where she'd recently lost two lower baby teeth.

Karin bent to plant a kiss on the top of her curly head. "And I love you. Lots."

Otto shut the hatch. He had all the grocery bags, two in each hand.

"I'll help, Grandpa!" Supergirl proclaimed. She planted her rain boots wide, stuck out her little chest and propped her fists on her hips. Otto set two of the bags on the garage floor, fished out a block of Swiss cheese from one and passed it to her. The cheese in one hand, both arms spread wide, cape rippling, Coco ran back up the stairs and into the house, slamming the door behind her.

"You gotta love that enthusiasm," said Otto as he bent to pick up the bags again. Karin just stood there staring down at his bent head. His hair was all white now and thinning, his pink scalp showing through at the crown. He met her eyes as he stood again. "What happened?" he asked quietly.

She replied in a small voice. "I saw Liam at Safeway."

"You tell him?" Her dad and her brother, Sten, and Sten's wife, Madison, knew that Liam was the baby's father. Sten and Otto had been after Karin for months to tell the man that he was going to be a dad. Madison mostly stayed out of it, though Liam was actually one of her long-lost brothers.

Karin stared into the middle distance, thinking of Madison for no particular reason. Sten's new bride had been switched at birth, of all impossible things. She'd met Sten when she came to Valentine Bay last March to find the family she'd just learned she had.

"Karin. You tell Liam?" her dad asked for the second time.

She blinked and made herself answer the question. "Uh. I did. Yes. I told him."

"And?"

"And I said I was going straight home, that if he wanted to talk about it, I'll be here."

"You're thinking he'll be coming by, then?"

She nodded. "And soon, would be my guess. If you could maybe keep the kids downstairs...?" The house was really two complete houses in one. Karin, her dad and the kids lived on the first floor just above the garage. Sten and Madison had the upper floor when they were in town, which they weren't right now. Madison was a bona fide movie star. Currently, she and Sten spent most of their time in LA or on location wherever she was filming.

"No problem," said Otto. "I'll keep an eye on the kids and send Liam up when he gets here."

On the top floor of the house, in Sten's quiet kitchen, Karin brewed a cup of raspberry leaf tea. As she waited for it to steep, she stood at the slider that opened onto the wide upper deck and watched the layers of clouds over the water. The waves slid into shore and retreated, leaving the wet sand smooth as glass in their wake.

"Karin." Liam spoke from directly behind her.

She stiffened in surprise and turned to face him. His hair was kind of standing on end and his eyes had a haunted look. "Hey. I, um, didn't hear you come in."

He stared at her for several seconds with a numbly disbelieving expression on his face before he finally said, "Your dad. He told me to just go up."

"That's fine. Great. Let's sit down, why don't we?" She gestured toward the sitting area.

"No, thanks." He blinked at her. "I'd rather stand."

"Maybe some tea or something?"

"No. Nothing." He turned on his heel and strode away from her. When he reached the hallway that led to the bedrooms, he turned again and came back, halting in the same place he'd been before he stalked off. "You're pregnant."

Hadn't they already covered that? "Yes, I am."

"I can't… I don't…" It was just like at Safeway. The poor man seemed incapable of completing a sentence. "I mean, uh, you said it was…"

"Yours, Liam," she gently confirmed again. "Yes. The baby is yours."

"And you're due…?"

"In a week."

"A week." The wild state of his hair made more sense as he put both hands to his head, got two fistfuls of hair and pulled. "Mine. Wow. Mine." And off he went again, his long legs carrying him swiftly past the table, on through the sitting area to the hallway that led to the bedrooms. Next to the hallway, stairs led down to the lower floor. For a moment, he just stood there, his head going back and forth, as though he couldn't decide whether to run down the stairs or set off along the hallway.

Karin didn't know what to do, either, so she just waited by the slider. Eventually, he turned and came toward her again.

"A week," he repeated when he stopped a foot away from her. "I'll be a dad in a week is what you just said."

Excuses weren't going to cut it. She offered them anyway. "I'm so sorry, Liam. I was going to tell you earlier, but I didn't really even know where to start. And there's not much you could do at this point, anyway. So I thought I would just wait until after the birth."

"You thought you would just wait…"

"Yes. Liam, I promise you, there's no pressure. You can think it over, decide how much involvement you want to have." Okay, yeah. No matter what he decided, eventually, she would be after him to spend a little time with his child. And he would have to cough up some child support, too. But it felt beyond rude to hit the poor guy with all that today when he seemed so completely torn up to learn there was a baby on the way.

"No pressure," he echoed blankly.

"That's right. There's no big rush to make decisions. Truly, you can just take your time, figure out what works for you."

He raked his hair back with both hands. "But… married, maybe? We should get—"

"What? Wait." Now she was the one frantically blinking. "Married? Us?"

"Well, uh, yeah."

She needed to nip that terrible idea right in the bud. "No, Liam. Don't be silly. Of course not." No way was she getting married just because there was a baby coming. Been there, done that. Bought the T-shirt, saw the movie. Lived through the heartbreak. Never. Again.

And dear God in heaven, could she have made a bigger mess of this?

"Listen," she said. "After the birth we'll do DNA. You'll have plenty of time to deal with this. You really will—and you know, you look awful. Liam, come on. You need to sit down." She reached for his arm.

He jerked away before she could make contact. "I'll stand." They just stared at each other.

She cast desperately about for something meaningful to say. "Liam, I really am so sorry to—"

"Stop." He actually showed her the hand.

And then he spun on his heel again and paced off toward the stairs, shaking his head as he went, turning right back around and coming toward her once more, halting stock-still a few feet from where she waited. He looked wrecked, ruined, but he held his broad shoulders straight and proud. "Last March, when you broke it off with me, did you know you were pregnant then?"

She wanted to lie to him, make herself look a fraction less like a complete jerk for the way she'd handled the situation. But she didn't lie. "Yeah. I knew then."

His forehead crinkled in a frown. "You broke it off, but you didn't bother to tell me you were having my kid?"

"I felt awful. I couldn't make myself admit to you that we were having a baby. I mean, why me? How many women have you been with?"

He fell back a step. "What's that got to do with anything?"

"Liam. I know you. I grew up with you. We were in the same grade at school. We even went on two dates in high school, remember?"

"Of course, I remember."

"My, um, point is, you're hot and easy to be with. The women have always loved you and you have loved them right back. How many of those women did you get pregnant?"

"Karin." He was pulling his hair again. So strange to see him like this, at a loss. Undone. "Come on, now. Where is this going?"

"The answer is none of them, right—not until me?"

Now he looked worried. "Why do I feel like anything I say right now is going to be wrong?"

"Oh, please. No. You are not wrong. This is not your fault—it's not my fault, either, though. Or at least, that's what I keep telling myself. But I also can't help asking myself, why does the condom fail only for *me*? Why couldn't *I* have sense enough to get back on the pill—or better yet, get a contraceptive implant? But every time you and I got together, I really thought it would be the last time. What was the point, I asked myself? I wouldn't be having sex with anyone again anytime soon. But then I would get a free evening and I would remember how you said to give you a call anytime—I mean, think about it. Four times, we got together."

That first time had been last December, at Christmastime. Then there'd been once in January, once in February and that last time in March. The first time, she'd promised herself it would be the only time. The second time, too. And that was the one where the condom must have failed.

After that, it hadn't mattered anyway, whether she got herself an implant or not.

"Four times together," she muttered, "and *this* happens." She looked down and shook her head at her protruding belly. "What is the matter with me, to do that to you?"

"Uh, Karin, I—"

"No, really. You don't have to answer that. It's not a question that even needs an answer. And I swear I was going to tell you about the baby that last time, in March. I saw that last night as my chance to let you know what was happening..." She ran out of breath. But he only kept on staring.

So she sucked in another breath and babbled on. "When I called you that night in March, I swear it was my plan to tell you. But then, well, you kissed me and I kissed you back and I thought how much I wanted you and how long it was likely to be before I ever had sex with a man again. I thought, *one more time*, you know? I thought, *what can it hurt*?"

Still, he said nothing.

She couldn't bear the awful silence, so she kept right on talking. "I promised myself I would tell you afterward, but then afterward came, and the words? They *wouldn't* come and then I started thinking that you didn't need to know for months. Liam, I messed up, okay? I messed up and then I didn't reach out and the longer I didn't, the harder it got. And now, well..." She lifted her arms out the sides. "Here we are."

He just continued to look at her through disbelieving eyes. For a really long time. She longed to open her mouth again and fill the silence with the desperate sound of her own voice. But she'd already jabbered out that endless and completely unhelpful explanation of essentially nothing. Really, what more was there to add to all the ways she'd screwed up?

He broke the silence. "I have to leave now."

She felt equal parts relieved—and desolate. "Okay."

"But I will be back."

"Of course."

"We'll talk more."

What was she supposed to say to that? "Sure. Whenever you're ready."

"Okay. Soon." And then he was striding away from her for the fourth time.

She watched as he vanished into the stairwell and didn't move so much as a muscle until she heard his car start up outside and drive away. After that, for several grim seconds, she thought she might cry, just bawl her eyes out because she felt so terrible about everything and she'd done such a crap job of telling poor Liam he had a baby on the way.

The tears never came, though. Eventually, she turned around and stared blindly out at the ocean for a while.

By the time she remembered her raspberry leaf tea, it was cold.

Chapter Two

Liam got halfway to the gorgeous house he'd built for himself in nearby Astoria before he realized that he needed to talk to his oldest brother Daniel.

Years ago, when their parents died, Daniel, eighteen at the time, essentially took over as the head of the Bravo family. He became a second father to all of them. Daniel was only four years older than Liam. Didn't matter. When Liam needed fatherly advice, he usually sought out his oldest brother.

He called Daniel's cell from the car.

"Where are you?" Liam demanded when Daniel picked up.

"Hi to you, too. I'm at the office." Daniel ran the family business, Valentine Logging. "What do you need?"

"Long story. I'll be there in ten."

"Good enough."

Valentine Logging had its headquarters on the Warrenton docks between Valentine Bay and Astoria. Liam parked in front of the hangar-like building that housed the offices.

Daniel was waiting. He ushered Liam into his private office, shut the door and gestured toward the sitting area on one side of the room. "You look like hell. What's going on?"

"I need to talk." Liam sank to the leather sofa. "You know Karin Killigan?"

"Of course." Daniel dropped into the club chair.

"Karin and me, we had a thing last winter."

Daniel frowned. "Wait a minute—Karin's pregnant, right?"

"Yeah. How did you know?" Did everyone know but him?

"Keely told me." Keely was Daniel's wife.

"How did Keely know?"

"She hung out a little with Karin at Madison and Sten's wedding. According to Keely, Karin was noticeably pregnant then—but you missed the wedding, right?"

"Right." He'd felt bad to miss it, but he'd had a work conflict in Portland, one he couldn't put off or get out of.

Liam owned Bravo Trucking, which he'd built up from a few rigs that hauled strictly for Valentine Logging into a fleet with over two hundred trucks and two hundred fifty employees. His original terminal was nearby, right there in Warrenton. Last year, he'd opened one in Portland, too.

Daniel was leaning forward again. "Are you saying the baby is yours?"

"Yeah." The word scraped his throat as he said it. "Karin says she's been trying for months to work up the nerve to tell me. I probably still wouldn't know if I hadn't seen her coming out of Safeway a couple of hours ago." And he had that feeling again, like if he sat still, he might just lose his mind. So he jumped up, paced to the door and then paced back again.

Daniel said, "You never mentioned you were dating Karin."

"Dating?" He stopped by Daniel's chair. "I wouldn't call it dating. It was only a few times, whenever she could get away. She wanted it kept just between the two of us. I agreed it would be the way she wanted it and I never told anyone else that we were hooking up."

"Liam," Daniel said quietly. "Sit back down. Come on, man. It's all going to work out."

He dropped to the couch again. "I guess I'm kind of in shock."

Daniel got up. "Scotch or water?"

Liam braced his elbows on his spread knees and put his head in his hands. "Neither. Both." Dropping his hands from his face, he flopped back against the cushions and stared up at the ceiling.

Daniel asked, "Didn't you and Karin date in high school?"

"Briefly." Liam shut his eyes. "I always thought Karin was cute, you know? Senior year, she asked me to a Sadie Hawkins dance. We had a great time. I took her out to a show a couple of weeks later. But when she started hinting that she wanted to be exclusive with me, I told her what I told all the girls, that I didn't do virgins and I wasn't getting serious with anyone. Ever."

"Classy," remarked Daniel wryly. "And I'm guessing that was it for you and Karin in high school."

Liam let out a grunt in the affirmative. "When we met up last December, it was so great to reconnect with her. She's smart. She takes zero crap, you know? A guy can't get ahead of her. Better-looking than ever, too, with those gorgeous eyes that look blue at first glance but are actually swirled with green and gray. Plus, she has all that wild, dark hair. And her attitude is seriously snarky. She's fun." He couldn't help recalling the shock and guilt on her face when he'd stopped her at Safeway. "Not so snarky today, though. She really felt bad, that she'd waited so long to tell me…"

"Here you go."

Liam opened his eyes. Daniel stood over him, a bottle of water in one hand, a glass with two fingers of amber liquid in the other. "Thanks." Liam set down the glass on the side table and took a long drink from the water bottle. "I should go." He drank the rest of the water and set the empty bottle by the untouched glass of Scotch.

"Hold on," said Daniel. "I thought you said you needed to talk."

"I did talk." He rose and clapped his brother on the shoulder. "Thanks for listening."

Liam's new house in Astoria was four thousand square feet and overlooked the Columbia River. He'd had a decorator in to furnish it in a sleek, modern style, lots of geometric patterns and oxidized oak, pops of deep color here and there.

As a rule, coming home made him feel pretty good about everything. He had a thriving business, a fat bank account and a gorgeous house. By just about any standards, he'd made a success of his life so far.

Today, though, a big house and money in the bank didn't feel all that satisfying. He was going to be a dad.

Just like that. Out of the blue—at least, that was how it felt to him.

Karin had kept saying that he didn't have to do anything right now.

Wrong.

He needed to do *something*. He just didn't really know what.

Maybe he should call Deke Pasternak. Deke was in family law. A little legal advice couldn't hurt about now, could it?

The lawyer answered on the second ring. "Hey. Liam. Good to hear from you. How've you been?"

"I just found out I'm going to be a father. Baby's due in a week."

Usually a fast talker, Deke took several seconds to reply. "Well. Congratulations?" He said it with a definite question mark at the end.

Two could play that game. "Thanks?"

"So… You want to meet for a drink or something?"

"How about a phone consultation?"

Five slow beats of complete silence, after which Deke asked, "You okay, man?"

"I'm working on it. Just bill me for this call and tell me what you think."

Deke did some throat-clearing. "What I think?"

"Yeah."

"About your being a dad?"

"That's right."

"Are you asking as a friend or do you want my legal opinion?"

"You're billing me, aren't you?"

"Uh, sure. So this isn't anyone you were dating seriously, then?"

Liam thought of Karin again, standing there by the

sliding glass door in her brother's empty kitchen, looking miserable. "Why does that matter?"

"Let me put it this way, how did you find out that the baby's yours?"

"She told me."

"Ah. Right there. That could be a problem."

"Well, she should have told me sooner, yeah. She admitted that."

"No, Liam. What I mean is, what she told you proves nothing."

"She's seriously pregnant, man. I saw her with my own eyes."

"Not what I'm getting at. I'm trying to say that before you take *her* word for it, you need to let me arrange for DNA testing. It's best to clear up any doubts right out of the gate. I hate to say it, but it's a possibility that this baby isn't even yours."

Liam had always been an easygoing sort of guy. He never got worked up about anything. But hearing Deke Pasternak imply that Karin Killigan had lied to him about her baby being his? That just pissed him the hell off. "You're way off base there, Deke. She already mentioned a DNA test, as a matter fact. She's a straight-ahead woman and she's not trying to trap me."

"I'm just trying to help you."

"No. Uh-uh. You don't know this woman."

"Well, I—"

"She would never try to trap a man—she's so independent, she called off our relationship before I could figure out a way to convince her that we should even have a relationship. She wasn't even going to *tell* me about the baby until after the birth. I think she would have put off sharing the big news with me forever if that had been an option for her. But she's a good woman and that wouldn't be right. So, no. If she says the baby's mine, it's mine, damn it."

"Liam. Come on. Don't get me wrong. I'm not disrespecting the, her, mother of your child."

"Yeah? Coulda fooled me."

"I only meant that it's important to prove paternity once and for all. You need to get irrefutable proof and proceed from there. You do that, you know where you stand. And when you know where you stand, you can decide what to do next."

Why was he even talking to Deke? The guy had always irritated him. "You just don't get it, do you, Deke? I'm going to be a *father*. Like in a week! I have no clue how to be someone's dad." True, in the past year or so, he *had* been thinking that it was time for him to start considering having a family of his own.

But not in a week, for crying out loud!

"I'm sorry, Liam. But I don't really think it's legal advice you're looking for here."

Liam had to agree with that. "You're right. Gotta go. Have a good one, Deke."

"You, too. Ping me anytime you—" Deke was still talking as Liam hung up.

He dropped his phone on the sofa table, took off his boots and stretched out on the couch. That lasted maybe thirty seconds, at which point he realized that no way could he keep still.

Sitting up again, he put his Timberlands back on.

He needed to…know stuff. A lot was expected of a guy as a dad. Witness Daniel, for example. Married at nineteen with three brothers and four sisters to raise. And now he had twins from his first wife, Lillie, who'd died shortly after the twins' birth. Twins, and a daughter with his second wife, Keely.

The responsibilities never ended for a guy like Daniel. He worked all day and then went home to a wife, a couple of three-year-olds, a nine-month-old baby girl and their youngest sister Grace, who hadn't moved out on her own yet. Daniel made it all look pretty effortless, mostly—or at least, he had since he and Keely got together. He was a happy man now.

Liam could learn a lot from Daniel. He really shouldn't have just jumped up and run out of his brother's office like that. He had a million questions and Daniel would be the one to answer them.

However, to get advice from Daniel, he would be required to sit still and listen. That wasn't happening. Not now, not today.

Grabbing his phone and the jacket he'd shucked off when he entered the house, he headed out again—back to Valentine Bay and Valentine Bay Books down in the historic district, where the fortyish blonde clerk greeted him with a big smile. "How can I help you?"

"I'm having a baby. It's my first and I need to know everything."

"Well, of course you do." She led the way to the baby and childcare section and recommended a few books on first-time fatherhood.

He grabbed those. "I'm just going to look around for a while."

She left him to it. An hour later, he'd chosen more than twenty new-dad and baby books. After all, he had a lot to learn. And that could take a lot of books.

Back at home, he stuck a frozen pizza in the oven and sat down to begin his education in fatherhood.

At two on Saturday morning, he was still reading. Not long after that, he must have dropped off to sleep. He woke to daylight at his breakfast nook table with his head resting on *The Expectant Father: The Ultimate Guide for Dads-to-Be*.

He made coffee, had a shower and called both of his offices, where for once everything seemed to be rolling along right on schedule.

At a little after nine, he was knocking on the door of the house on Sweetheart Cove, a bag of baby books in one hand—just the ones he thought had the most to offer, in case he needed to refer to the experts while discussing his upcoming fatherhood with Karin.

Karin's daughter answered the door. She was a cute little thing with big blue eyes and curly hair in pigtails.

"You came yesterday, didn't you?" the child demanded at the sight of him.

"That's right, I did."

"Grandpa told us to stay in the great room when you came, but I peeked." Her little mouth drew down at the corners in a puzzled frown. "Who *are* you?"

Otto Larson appeared from the living area. He wore a patient smile. "Coco, this is Liam Bravo. Invite him in."

"Come *in*, Liam Bravo." She swept out an arm in the general direction of the arch that led to the downstairs living area.

"Thank you, Coco." He stepped into the foyer.

"You're welcome."

Liam shut the door as Coco darted to her grandfather and tugged on his hand. Otto bent close and she whispered in his ear.

He gave Liam a wink. "Yep. Liam is one of *those* Bravos. Your Aunt Madison is his sister."

"I knew it!" crowed Coco. She aimed a giant smile at Liam, one that showed a gap where she'd lost a couple of lower teeth. "Aunt Madison is my *friend* and we have to be careful and not talk about her to most people because she is a movie star and she needs her *privacy*. But since you're her brother, I can say what I want about Madison to you."

Liam made a noise in the affirmative.

Coco Killigan chattered on. "I'm seven and I go to second grade. I have two best friends in my class and for Halloween, I will be Jewel from *101 Dalmatians*." Coco pointed at the bag of books dangling from his left hand. "You brought books. I like books."

"Coco," said Otto fondly. "I think Liam's here to talk to your mom."

Coco giggled. "Okay!" and skipped away through the arch into the other room.

"Come on," said Otto. "I'll get Karin." He turned and led the way into the first-floor living area, where a boy a couple of years older than Coco sat at the table with a laptop, a paper notepad and a stack of schoolbooks. Otto introduced the boy as Ben, Karin's son.

"Nice to meet you," said Ben, sounding much older than his nine or ten years. He had straight brown hair and serious brown eyes.

As Liam tried to think of what to say to him, Karin spoke from behind him.

"Liam."

He turned to her. She wore jeans and a long, ribbed sweater that clung to the front of her, accentuating her enormous belly. Her wild hair was pinned up in a sloppy little bun. She wore no makeup and the shadows under her eyes made her look tired—tired and soft and huggable, somehow. He wanted to wrap his arms around her and bury his nose in the curve of her neck, find out if she still smelled as good as he remembered.

"I wasn't expecting you." She didn't seem all that happy to see him.

Too bad. He was going to be around. A lot. She would need to get used to that. "I said I'd be back."

She glanced past him, at Otto. "Dad, I'll just take Liam on upstairs?"

"Fine with me," the older man replied.

She focused on Liam again and pasted on a tight smile. "This way..."

Liam followed her back into the foyer and up to the empty top floor, where she offered him a seat in the living area.

He took the sofa and set the bag of books at his feet.

"So, how are you doing?" Karin lowered herself into one of the chairs.

He had so many things to say and no idea where to start. "Uh. Good. Fine. Really. I talked to my lawyer."

"Well, that's good." She gave an uncomfortable little laugh. "I think..."

Now she looked worried—and he didn't blame her. Seriously? Deke? He had to go and mention Deke? Nothing good was going to come of telling her what Deke said. "He, um, wasn't helpful, but the point is I'm realizing that everything is workable. You need to know that I will provide child support—and I've read a little about parenting plans. We'll get one of those."

"That's great." She sat with her knees pressed tightly together, like someone waiting for an appointment she wasn't looking forward to.

He leaned in. "I also want you to know I'm here for you, Karin. Whatever you need, I'll make sure that you get it."

She nodded at him, an indulgent sort of nod, like he was her seven-year-old daughter, or something. He felt a flare of annoyance, that she so easily categorized him as someone she didn't have to take too seriously.

The annoyance quickly faded as he realized he missed her—missed the *real* Karin, the woman who kissed him like she couldn't get enough of the taste of him, the one who was always ready with some wiseass remark.

He wanted the real Karin back.

He also wanted her to learn to count on him, to trust him, though he'd never been the sort of guy who was willing to work to gain a woman's trust.

But he'd never been almost a father before, either.

Somehow, impending fatherhood changed everything. She was the mother of his child and he wanted her, wanted to be with her, to take care of her.

One way or another, he would get what he wanted.

Karin wasn't sure she liked the way Liam was looking at her. It was a thoughtful kind of look, a measuring look. It was also intimate, somehow.

He was a beautiful man, all golden and deep-chested, with hard arms and proud shoulders. It would be so good, to have those arms around her, to rest against that strong chest. Looking at him now, in the gray light of this chilly fall morning, she couldn't help wishing…

No.

Never mind.

Bad idea.

She and Liam weren't a couple and they never would be.

"So," she said to break the lengthening silence between them, "What's with the bag of books?"

"Research." He granted her a proud smile. "You know, first-time fatherhood, pregnancy, labor and delivery. All that. I've got a lot to catch up on and I've been doing my homework. I stayed up late trying to get a handle on all the stuff I need to know."

He was too sweet. He really was.

She'd been awake half the night, too, feeling bad about everything. And now she sat across from him waiting for him to get thoroughly pissed off at her—that she'd gotten pregnant in the first place when he used a condom every time. That she didn't bust to the baby when she broke it off with him and then, for all those months and months, that she'd never once reached out to let him know he was going to be a dad. He probably wondered if she ever *would* have told him.

And frankly, if he hadn't spotted her at the supermarket yesterday, she had no idea when she would have pulled up her big-girl panties and gotten in touch with the guy.

They stared at each other across the endless expanse of Sten's coffee table. Liam looked like he had a million things to tell her—tender things. Kind things. Helpful things.

The man truly wasn't angry. Not yet, anyway. He was sweet and sincere and he just seemed to want to be there for her and for the baby, to do the right thing.

His kindness reminded her sharply of how much she'd liked him when they met up again last year. In addition to his general charm and hotness, Liam Bravo, high school heartbreaker, had grown up to be a good man.

And right now, that just made her want to cry.

He said, "I was thinking…"

"Yeah?"

"Looking back on that night in March when you broke it off, I knew there was something weighing on your mind. I should have tried harder to get you to open to me."

She couldn't believe he'd just said that. "Liam. You were great. Don't you dare blame yourself."

"Look, I just need to know what *you* need."

"I'm good, I promise. Everything's pretty much ready. We're just waiting for the baby to come."

He frowned in a thoughtful sort of way. "Have you been going to childbirth classes?"

"I took the classes, yes. Like I said, I'm ready."

"A labor coach?" he asked and then clarified, "Do you have one?"

"I have two, as a matter of fact—Naomi and Prim." Naomi Khan Smith and Primrose Hart Danvers had been her best friends since kindergarten. Both women were married now. Naomi had two boys.

"Prim and Naomi. Makes sense." He'd grown up with her BFFs, same as she had. "And even though I get that you're all set and Prim and Naomi will take good care of you, I want to be there, when the baby comes."

She tried not to picture him standing beside her while she sweated and groaned with her legs spread apart. If he wanted to be there, he had the right. "Yes. That's fine. Great."

"So you'll call me, when you go into labor?"

"I will, absolutely."

Liam had a million more things to discuss with the soon-to-be mother of his child. But sitting here across from her in Sten Larson's too-quiet great room, he couldn't seem to remember a single one of them.

She just looked so brave and uncomfortable—and alone. Beyond being smart and good-looking and self-reliant, there was something that hurt his heart about Karin Killigan, something walled-off and sad.

"What else?" she asked. He knew she was trying not to sound impatient, but it was obvious to him that she couldn't wait for him to leave.

And why stay? She didn't really want him here, there was nothing he could do for her at the moment—and he hated the feeling that he contributed to her sadness.

"Nothing else—not right now, anyway," he heard himself say.

She stood, a surprisingly agile move given the size of her belly. "Well, all right then. Come by anytime. I mean that. Or call. Whatever."

"Thanks." He grabbed his bag of books and followed her down to the lower floor.

Her little girl stuck her curly head into the foyer as Karin was showing him out the door. "Bye, Liam Bravo."

"Bye, Coco."

"Can I call you just Liam?"

When he glanced at the silent woman beside him, she shrugged. "Up to you."

He gave Coco a smile. "Just Liam works for me."

"Okay! Bye, Liam. You can come and see me anytime." Coco waved as Karin ushered him out the door.

Liam went back to Astoria and had breakfast at a homey little diner he liked. From there, he went on to his office at the Warrenton terminal and put in a half day of work.

That evening, he drove the few miles to Valentine Bay and stopped at the Sea Breeze on Beach Street for a beer. His baby sister Grace was behind the bar. She served him his favorite IPA and asked him if something was bothering him.

"It's all good," he lied and Gracie left him alone except to give him a refill when he signaled for it. He sat there sipping his beer, feeling kind of gloomy, going back and forth over whether or not to just tell his youngest sister that he was about to be a dad. At some point, he would have to break the big news to the whole family.

Soon, actually. The baby would be here in no time at all.

It all felt so strange. Completely unreal. He still had no clue how he was going to do it—be a dad.

But he wasn't giving up. Uh-uh. Karin and her sad eyes weren't keeping him away. He would be there for her and for his kid whether she wanted him around or not.

"Is Liam your boyfriend, Mommy?" Coco took a big sip of her milk and then set the glass carefully down. She picked up her fork and speared a clump of mac and cheese with ham.

Karin and her dad shared a glance across the dinner table. Otto lifted one bushy eyebrow. Karin read that look: *it's as good a time as any.*

She cast a sideways glance at Ben. He was watching her, wearing what she always thought of as his Little Professor look. Serious. Thoughtful. Ben never just burst out with things the way Coco did. He watched. He waited. He made carefully considered, responsible decisions.

"As a matter of fact," Karin said to her daughter, "I've been meaning to talk to both you and Ben about Liam."

"I like Liam!" Coco speared a green bean and stuck it in her mouth.

Dear God. Where to even start? "I like Liam, too," Karin said, trying to sound relaxed and natural and feeling anything but. "And several months ago, I…went out with him."

Ben's forehead scrunched up the way it always did when some complex math problem didn't compute. "You were dating Liam?"

Not dating, exactly. "Uh, yes. I was. We're not, um, dating anymore, though. But we are friends. And that's a good thing. Because, as it turns out…" Was she blowing this? Most likely. She forged on anyway. "We will all probably be seeing a lot more of Liam because he is the new baby's father."

Ben said nothing.

Coco was incredulous. She set down her fork. "*Our* baby's father?"

"Yes." It was official. She was a terrible mother who needed lessons in how to share awkward, confusing information with her own children. "Liam is our baby's dad."

Coco frowned. "Is he going to come and live in our house?"

"No, honey."

"But doesn't he want to be with the baby?"

"Yes. Yes, he does. And he will be here often to see the baby. And when the baby gets older, the baby will probably stay with Liam some of the time."

"Oh," said Coco, and picked up her fork again. "Okay." She stabbed herself another big bite of mac and cheese.

Karin glanced across at her dad again. He gave her a shrug and a reassuring smile.

Ben, who understood the mechanics of reproduction, asked the question she'd been dreading. "How come you didn't say who the baby's dad was when I asked you before?" He'd asked several months ago, not long after she'd made the announcement that he and Coco would have a new brother or sister.

Because I'm a lily-livered scaredy-cat, she thought. She said, "Well, sweetheart, as I said then, I wanted to talk to the baby's dad first."

"You took a long time to talk to him."

Ouch. "Yes, I did. I'm sorry about that, I really am."

Ben tipped his head to the side, pondering. "Why? Were you nervous, to tell him?"

Understatement of the decade. "I was, yes."

"But now he knows and he's happy that he'll be a dad?"

"I haven't asked him that question. But he seems very determined to be a *good* dad."

Ben was still looking kind of troubled over the whole situation.

But Coco wasn't. "Our baby will like having Liam for a dad," she declared. "Liam's nice—and I finished my dinner. What's for dessert?"

Otto chuckled. "I think there might be a full carton of chocolate ice cream in the freezer."

Karin brushed Ben's arm. "Want to go talk about this in the other room, just the two of us?"

Ben shook his head. "Thanks, Mom. I'd rather just have some dessert."

On Sunday, Karin went in to work at Larson Boatworks, the boat-building and refitting company her dad had started thirty-five years before. Karin ran the office.

That day, her dad kept an eye on the kids at home

so she could spend several hours tying up loose ends on the job before the baby came. When she got back to the Cove late that afternoon, her dad reported that Liam had dropped by.

"Should I call him?" she asked.

"He didn't say to ask you to."

"Did he mention what he needed to talk to me about?"

Her dad gave her a look, indulgent and full of wry humor. "I'm not sure he *knows* what he needs to talk to you about."

For the rest of that day and into the evening, she kept thinking that she probably ought to call Liam, check in, ask him if he had any questions or anything. Somehow, though, she never quite got around to picking up the phone.

Monday, her leave from work began. Her dad dropped the kids at the bus stop and then went on to work.

It was nice, having the house to herself. She took a half hour just deciding what to wear and ended up settling on a giant purple T-shirt dress with an asymmetrical hem.

Really, she didn't want jeans or leggings wrapped around her balloon of a belly today, so she settled on thigh-high socks in royal blue with her oldest, comfiest pair of Doc Martens boots on her feet.

Once she was dressed, she felt suddenly energized, so she vacuumed and dusted and rechecked the baby's room for the umpteenth time, making sure everything was ready. Around eleven, just as she finished assembling two large baking dishes of lasagna and sticking them in the freezer to reheat when needed, she heard the doorbell ring.

It was Liam. He had a pink teddy bear in one hand and a blue bear in the other.

"I forgot to ask. What are we having?" He smiled that killer smile of his, and she felt way too glad to see him.

She laughed. "It's a boy."

And just like that, he threw the pink bear over his shoulder and handed her the blue one.

The man was too charming by half. "Thank you—and I think we should save the pink one, too."

"Is there something you aren't telling me?" He pretended to look alarmed. "We're having twins, aren't we?"

"Oh, God, no. I just meant it seems wrong to leave it lying there on the front step."

He went and got the pink bear. "Fine. The baby gets two bears."

It seemed only right to offer, "Would you like to see his ultrasound pictures?"

"I thought you'd never ask."

She ushered him in. As he brushed past her, she got a hint of his cologne, a scent of leather and sandalwood that caused a sudden, stunning remembrance of the two of them all those months ago, naked on tangled sheets.

He paused in the arch to the living area and glanced back at her. "Something wrong?"

"Not a thing." She shut the door and followed him into the first-floor living area.

In the kitchen, she put the blue bear down on the counter. He set the pink one beside it as she went to the double-doored fridge, which was covered with family pictures and artwork created by both Ben and Coco. "Here we are." She took the two ultrasound shots from under a strawberry magnet and handed them over. "These were at eighteen weeks."

He studied them. "Wait. Is that…?" He slanted her a grin.

"What sharp eyes you have, Liam Bravo. Yep. A bona fide penis—and I have a video of that same procedure. Want to see it?"

"Oh, yeah."

She stuck the pictures back on the fridge and led him to the table where she'd left her laptop. He laughed in a sort of startled wonder as he watched his son wave his tiny arms and feet, yawn and suck his thumb.

After he'd seen the whole thing through twice, he glanced up at her. "You said you were all ready for him. Does that mean he has a room and everything?"

She grabbed the two teddy bears and gestured toward the hallway to the bedrooms. "Right this way." He followed her as she explained, "We're lucky this house has so many rooms, including five bedrooms on this level. I had a sort of craft room/home office in one." She led him to the end of the hall where the door stood open. "Ta-da!" She put the bears on the dresser by the door.

"Wow." Liam seemed really pleased.

And out of nowhere, she was recalling one of the depressing fights she'd had with Ben, Sr., before Ben was born.

Bud, as everyone always called him, had kept promising to help her paint the tiny closet of a spare room at the apartment they'd shared back then.

Somehow, though, he never found the time to keep his promise. Bud had loved the life of a commercial fisherman and he was always out on a boat, working the fisheries up and down the Pacific coast, from Southern California to Alaska. He just kept saying "later," every time she tried to pin him down as to when, exactly, he would put in some time on the baby's room.

In the end, she fixed up the room herself, though not until after they'd had a doozy of an argument over it— one in which they both said a lot of things they shouldn't have. It was always like that with her and Bud. They would argue bitterly.

And then Bud would go off to work and be gone for weeks.

In the end, she'd tackled the nursery nook alone. When Bud came home, she showed him the finished product. He'd waved a dismissing hand and said it looked "fine" in a dead voice that communicated way too clearly how trapped he felt.

Liam's voice drew her back to the present. "The mural is amazing."

Covering the whole wall behind the crib, the mural included a snowcapped mountain, a starry night sky, an airplane sailing by the moon and tall evergreens standing sentinel off to one side, everything in grays, greens and silvers.

"Northwest outdoorsy," Liam said. "I like it a lot."

She rubbed her belly. The baby was riding really low and she'd had some contractions.

He was watching her. "You okay?"

"I'm fine. This baby is coming *soon*."

His eyes got bigger and he straightened from his easy slouch in the doorway. "As in now?"

She waved a hand and chuckled, thinking that this visit was going pretty well and she was glad about that. "Relax. Probably not today."

"Whew." He gazed at the mural again. "You paint that wall yourself?"

"More or less. Stencils. You can't beat 'em."

He shifted his gaze to her. He had a way of studying her, like he was memorizing the lines of her face.

He used to do that months ago, sitting across from her at whatever bar they met up in, or later, naked in bed. One night, she'd teased that he should take a picture. He'd promptly grabbed his phone off the table by the bed and aimed it at her, snapping off two shots.

She'd demanded he delete them, because who needs naked pictures of herself on a guy's phone?

He'd handed her the phone. She'd seen then that he'd only taken close-ups of her face. And when she glanced up at him, he gazed back at her so hopefully, like it would just be the greatest thing in the world, to have a couple of shots of her grinning, with total bed-head. She'd agreed he could keep the pictures—and then grabbed him close for a long, smoking-hot kiss.

Liam was still watching her. "Have you chosen a name for this baby boy of ours?"

"No, I have not. I kind of thought you might want input on his name."

Apparently, that was the right answer because he granted her a beautiful smile. "Thanks. I'll be thinking about names. I'll make up a list of ones I like. We can talk it over." Solemnly, he added, "I read all about baby daddies. I don't want to be that guy."

Her heart felt like someone was squeezing it. She hardly knew what to say. "You have *other* children?"

"Huh?" He seemed horrified. "No! Wait. I get it. You mean 'baby daddy' as in a flaky guy who has kids by different women, but I wasn't so much referring to the multiple baby mamas aspect. I meant a flaky guy, yeah. But in this case, a guy with only one baby, a guy who's basically a sperm donor with minimal involve-ment—that's what I *don't* want to be. I want to be on board with this baby, available, helping out. I want to be *there*, you know? Tell me you know that." He seemed so intense suddenly, as though it really bothered him that she might not understand his sincerity about pitching in.

"Hey, really. It's going to be okay, Liam."

"I hope so."

"It really is. I know I dropped the ball in a big way by not telling you what was going on sooner. I should've pushed past all the crap going on in my head and gotten in touch."

He watched her way too closely. "What crap, exactly?"

Uh-uh. Not going there. "My point is, I promise you that we *will* work together. You don't have to freak out."

"I'm not freaking out," he said vehemently—and a bit freakily.

Was this all going south suddenly?

And just when they'd both seemed to be feeling more at ease around each other.

She kind of wanted to cry, which was probably just hormones. But still. She really did want to get along with him. "Okay. You're right. You're not freaking out and I shouldn't have even hinted that you were and I'm really, um…" Her already weak train of thought went right off the rails as she felt something shift inside her—a gentle shift, yet also a sudden one, a tiny *pop* of sensation deep within.

And then something was dripping along the inside of her thighs.

Frowning, she looked down, which was pointless. Her giant belly blocked her view and whatever was dripping down there, it was only a trickle. So far, her thigh-highs seemed to be absorbing it.

"Okay," said Liam. "Something's happened. What?"

She made herself look straight into his startled blue

eyes and she put real effort into speaking calmly. "My water just broke. Would you mind driving me to Memorial Hospital?"

Chapter Three

Even more stunned than he'd been for most of the past few days, Liam croaked out, "Drive you to the hospital? Yes! Yes, I can do that."

"Great." With a low groan, Karin gripped the crib rail and lowered her head.

"Karin, are you…?"

She put up her free hand. "Just a contraction. Hold on…"

He stood there in the doorway waiting, feeling completely useless, as she panted and groaned some more.

Finally, she let go of the crib rail and looked straight at him. "Where's my phone?"

"I think I spotted it on the kitchen counter?"

"Right." One hand under her enormous stomach, she lumbered toward him. He fell back from the doorway so she could get by and then trailed after her as she made for the main room.

In the kitchen, she snatched up the phone. "This'll only take a minute. I've got a group text all set up—to Naomi, Prim and my dad. All I need to do is hit Send." The woman amazed him. Was there anything she wasn't ready for? She poked at the phone. "There. I'll call my doctor on the way—now get me a bath towel. Try the hall bathroom, first door on the left. I'll meet you at the front door."

"A towel?" He just stood there gaping at her because somehow his feet had forgotten how to walk.

"You want me to leak amniotic fluid all over the seats of that fancy blue Supercrew pickup out in front?"

"Uh. No?"

"Then go."

That got him moving. He raced off and returned with the towel. She had a suitcase ready, just waiting in the hallway. He took the suitcase and helped her into her coat. She grabbed her purse from the table by the door and off down the outside stairs they went, pausing midway for her to weather another contraction.

At the truck, he threw the suitcase in back, spread the towel on the seat and helped her in. She was already on the phone with her doctor as he turned the pickup around and headed up the hill behind the house.

At Memorial, he learned that the doctor was on the way and they were ready for Karin. They whisked her into a labor and delivery suite and let Liam tag along.

Luckily, he'd studied up on what the father should do during the birth. He'd learned that his sole mission in the delivery room was to be a source of strength and support, to be as patient and attentive to his baby's mother as he possibly could.

He really tried to be that, even though when her girlfriends showed up, he was mostly relegated to staying out of the way as they stepped up on either side of her to comfort her and coach her through her contractions. They fed her ice chips and helped her to the bathroom when she needed it. The whole thing took hours, with the doctor in and out, the delivery nurses, too.

Once he asked if he could take pictures.

Naomi turned to him and spoke gently, "It's so great that you're here, Liam, but Karin doesn't want you taking pictures of her lady bits."

"I would never do that," he answered fervently. "Just…maybe of the baby and then maybe of Karin with the baby and then maybe I could hold him, too—I mean, after he gets here, of course?"

On the far side of Karin, Prim was stifling a giggle.

Naomi grabbed him in a hug. "Isn't he adorable?" she asked Karin and Prim as she let him go.

He was trying to decide whether or not his manly dignity had just been impugned when Karin said, "Of course you can take a few pictures with your son." She met his eyes directly and he knew she was remembering that night in February, when he'd snapped a shot of her in his bed and she'd assumed he'd gotten more than just her face.

"Terrific," he replied, suddenly just crazy happy, right there in the delivery room, crazy happy and sure that everything was going to work out fine, though exactly what "fine" entailed he had no clear idea.

Things got messy soon after that. There were fluids and a little blood and Karin's groans started to sound more like screams and angry shouts.

But then the baby's head was crowning and everything sped up. As soon as the little guy's shoulders emerged, it was all over. The rest of him slipped out quick and easy. He was so tiny and wrinkled and red, covered with sticky whitish goo, wailing as the doctor caught him and laid him in Karin's waiting arms. Naomi grabbed Liam and pulled him around to stand in front of her, right next to Karin and the naked infant on her chest.

On Karin's other side, Prim stepped back so the nurse could wipe some of the goo off the baby and the doctor could deal with the umbilical cord. All Liam could do was stand there and stare.

He'd never realized how much he wanted children.

Not until this moment, when he actually had one—yeah, he'd had vague yearnings in the past year, to get more serious about his life, to get married, start a family.

But only in a generalized sort of way.

Until today.

Today, he knew exactly what he wanted—to be a father to this perfect little miracle he and Karin had made.

"Take a picture, Liam," Karin teased softly as she stroked the baby's shoulder, her hand gliding down the fat little arm to the tiny fist. Instantly, the baby wrapped his itty-bitty fingers around her thumb and held on.

Liam got out his phone and snapped a few shots.

The nurse gave him a towel to put on his shoulder. She let him hold his son for the first time. That was amazing, though it didn't last long.

He passed Naomi his phone and she got a few pictures of him with the baby. Too soon, the nurse took the little guy back and gave him to Karin again and she nursed him for the first time. Liam thought maybe he should turn away, give her some privacy. But she didn't seem concerned and nobody else cared. He watched as his son latched right on and went to work, the fingers of his right hand resting on the upper slope of Karin's breast, opening and closing as he sucked.

Liam watched not only his newborn son, but his son's mother, too. He stared and marveled and thought how, from that first night they'd had together last Christmas, she'd been constantly keeping him at arm's distance, giving in to the attraction between them, yeah. But then, once the hot times were over, pushing him away.

And what about the last few days since he'd found out about the baby? She'd continually reminded him to take his time, think it over, figure out just how *involved* he wanted to be.

As though a man could choose his level of involvement when he became a father.

There was no choosing with something like this. When it came to fatherhood, a man needed to be all in.

And he was. *In* this. Going for it. All the way.

Okay, he got it. He knew he had no idea, really, what the hell he was doing. But he could learn. And he *would* learn. One way or another, he was making it work with Karin. He damn well would create a family with the mother of his child.

Last Friday, that first day he found out she was pregnant, he'd stuttered out a half-assed proposal of marriage. She'd said no before he even really got the words out.

No wasn't going to cut it.

She glanced up from the baby and into his eyes. "Liam?" She seemed alarmed. "What's wrong?"

"Not a thing." He felt so calm, so absolutely determined. He held her gaze, steady on. "Marry me, Karin," he said.

Karin was wasted, completely exhausted.

She'd done this twice before, yes. But experience

didn't make having a baby feel any less like pushing out a watermelon. She just wanted to lie there and nurse her newborn and be grateful that labor was over, thank you very much.

But no.

Liam had to go to the marriage place. Hadn't they already agreed that marriage was no solution to anything?

And did he have to be so sweet about it? Sweet and determined and handsome and even-tempered and so damn helpful.

Liam Bravo was a dream.

Someday, he would make some lucky woman very happy.

But that day was not today and that woman was not her. No way was she going to be the one that Liam Bravo married because he felt he had to.

After the ongoing disaster with poor Bud, she'd had this fantasy that someday, maybe, she would actually get it right. In that lovely, impossible illusion, she'd imagined finding a man who would love her just for her, and then fall in love with Ben and Coco, too. That man would marry her for love and love alone. Duty and obligation and doing the right thing wouldn't even enter into it.

Later, they would have a baby or two, maybe. Like normal people do.

As of now, she was reasonably certain her fantasy was never actually going to come true. But that didn't mean she would settle for less.

Liam was still standing right beside the bed, staring down at her and the baby as though he could *will* her to agree to his well-meaning but totally unacceptable proposal.

The doctor had left the room and the nurse and

Naomi and Prim had fallen dead silent the moment Liam said the *M* word.

"Would you all give Liam and me a moment alone?" Karin asked her suddenly speechless friends and the too-quiet nurse.

"Of course." The nurse gave her shoulder a pat.

And the three women filed out the door so fast you'd think there was a fire. Or maybe a gas leak.

"Liam…" Karin kissed her baby's head and shifted a fraction so he was settled more firmly at her breast.

The man beside her bent closer. He was so good-looking, with those fine blue eyes and that mouth that made her think of deep, wet kisses. He also just happened to be kind and thoughtful and determined. Everything a woman could ask for in a man.

"Just say yes," he commanded. "It will work out. We'll be happy, you'll see."

Was she even a tiny bit tempted?

Of course. She was a heterosexual single mom. What was *not* to adore about Liam Bravo? The guy was practically perfect—at least right now, as he stared down at his newborn son after the excitement and drama of birth. Blinded by the wonder of new life and eager to do right by his child and his child's mother, marriage would naturally seem like the only choice to him.

The resentment, the growing certainty that she'd trapped him, the longing to be free of her—all that would come later.

Except it wouldn't. Because she wasn't going to marry him. No way. "Liam, we've been over this."

He shook his golden head. "We haven't. The other day, you said no before I even got the question out."

"I'm sorry I didn't hear you out, but my answer wouldn't have changed no matter what you said or how convincing you were or how patiently I waited for you to finish saying it. I'm not getting married just because we have a baby together. I need you to believe me when I tell you that."

"Listen." He straightened and stuck his hands in his pockets. "Don't give me an answer right now. Take your time. Think about it."

"Liam, I've already—"

"Think about it." A thread of steel had crept into his tone.

She had no need to think about it. Zero. Zip. Nada. She'd already given him her answer. Twice now. But he wasn't listening and an argument right now wasn't going to be good for her, for him or, most important, for their baby, who'd just been ejected from the warm, quiet safety of her womb. "All right. We'll talk about it later. If you need to. But my answer won't change."

"Just tell me you'll think about it."

She gave him a nod, though she really shouldn't have. He might construe any positive gesture as encouragement. But right now, she would do just about anything to stop this pointless marriage talk.

"Thank you." Liam bent close again. He brushed her forehead with his big, warm hand and placed a sweet, light kiss where his palm had been. "Thank you for my son and for promising to keep an open mind about marriage."

An open mind? Uh-uh. Her mind was locked down and dead bolted on that subject.

But for right now, he could go ahead and refuse to accept what she'd told him twice. Eventually he'd get the message. She even dared to hope the day would come when he would be grateful to her for not taking advantage of him at this emotional time.

As for the touch of his lips on her skin, she shouldn't have liked that so much, shouldn't have let herself sigh just a little when he bent near.

Really, she shouldn't even have allowed that kiss, should have turned her head away when his fine lips descended. He was a wonderful guy and she needed to begin developing a strong coparenting relationship with him—one that wouldn't include kisses, not even on the forehead.

Today, though, was a special circumstance. She'd just given birth to his baby. Surely, this once, a kiss on the forehead couldn't hurt...

Per hospital policy, Karin stayed the night at Memorial. Her girlfriends left after she was all settled in a regular room in the postpartum unit.

Liam stayed on. Karin suggested more than once that he ought to go home, get some dinner and a good night's rest. He said he wasn't tired.

A nurse came in with the birth certificate forms. They hadn't chosen a name yet, so the nurse helped them fill out everything else and told them where to send the form when the name had been decided. The space for the baby's last name didn't go empty. Liam wrote "Bravo" in there and Karin didn't object. No, she wasn't going to marry the guy, but she was determined to be respectful of his place in their baby's life.

The nurse left and finally, at a little before seven, Liam went off to get something to eat in the cafeteria.

Not five minutes after he went out the door, her dad and the kids arrived to meet the new baby. Apparently, Otto had spoken to them about how to behave in the hospital. Coco was as enthusiastic as ever, but she kept her voice down and sat with her little hands folded in her lap, a wild-haired, blue-eyed, second-grade angel. Ben was just Ben—curious and serious, even more polite than usual.

They each held the baby and seemed to enjoy that.

"He's kind of red," remarked Ben. He looked up. "But that's normal. I read that newborns have thin skin and the red blood vessels can show through."

When Coco's turn to hold her baby brother came, Ben leaned close and gently touched his head. "Soft spots," he declared with a solemn little nod. "They are called fontanels and there is one in front and one in back of the skull so that the baby's head can be flexible when he's coming through the birth canal and also so that the brain can grow quickly, now that he's born."

"He is so cute," Coco said in a carefully controlled whisper. "But his nose is kind of squished."

Ben loftily explained that a flattened nose also tended to happen during birth. "It's a tight squeeze," he said to his sister. "But his nose will assume its normal shape over time."

Coco looked up, frowning. "Mommy, what's our baby's name?"

"We haven't decided yet," Karin answered with a smile. *Note to self—ask Liam if he's made that list.*

Otto took the baby from Coco and declared him absolutely perfect. He'd just returned him to Karin's arms when there was a tap on the half-open door.

Liam had returned. "Hey. Should I come back?"

"Liam!" Coco exclaimed—and then realized she'd almost shouted. She clapped her hand over her mouth briefly and then stage-whispered, "Hi."

"Come on in," said Otto. "I've got to get these kids home, anyway. Homework to do, baths to take."

Liam glanced at her for permission.

What could she say? She waved him forward.

A few minutes later, after Karin's dad had assured her that he'd reached Sten in LA and reported that the newest member of the family had arrived safe and sound, Otto herded the kids out the door.

Liam said, "I'll bet you're tired."

"Oh, maybe just a little…"

"I'll leave you alone. But can I hold him—just for a minute?"

Her heart kind of melted at the longing in his eyes. "Of course."

He came close and she handed the baby over. Liam adjusted the swaddled blanket around his little face.

Karin leaned back against the pillow. "I keep meaning to ask if you've thought about a name yet."

He gently rocked the blanketed bundle from side to side. "I really can't decide."

She shut her weary eyes. "Well, think about it. We need to call him something other than 'the baby'."

"Will do." And he started whispering—to the baby, she assumed. She couldn't hear what he said, but the soft sound of his voice was soothing and she was so tired…

When Karin woke, Liam was gone and the baby was asleep in the plastic bassinet beside her. She didn't learn until breakfast time that he'd spent the night in the waiting room.

"I stayed just in case you might need me," he said when he came in with a sausage and egg sandwich in one hand and a paper cup of coffee in the other. He had bags under his eyes and his hair was slicked back as though he'd used the hospital restroom to splash water on his face. "When will they release you?" he asked.

"Later this morning or this afternoon, after my doctor comes by to check on us and sign us out of here."

"I'll drive you to the Cove."

She shook her head. "My dad's coming. He'll have the baby seat all hooked up in the car, ready to go."

He sipped his coffee. "Right. I need a baby seat."

She couldn't help chuckling. "Most conscientious single dad. Ever. Like in the history of dads."

That gorgeous smile lit up his face. "Thank you." He toasted her with his paper cup. "I do my best."

After he ate, he held the baby again. When he handed the little boy back, he said regretfully, "I suppose I need to check in at work, maybe even go to my place and take a shower. But I'll see you both later on today."

"Sure. As I said, I don't even know for certain what time they'll release us."

"No problem. I'll see you soon." He kissed the baby on the cheek and left.

As it turned out, the doctor didn't come to release her until the afternoon. Otto got one of the moms to bring Ben home from soccer practice. He picked up Coco from school and brought her to the hospital with him. She chattered away as they put the baby in his car seat and headed home.

At the Cove, the garage beneath the cottage next door was wide open. Karin spotted the back end of Liam's F-150 Raptor parked inside. Back when they were hooking up, he drove a black Audi Q8. The pickup suited him better, she thought, a true guy's guy sort of vehicle.

Not that what car he drove mattered to her in the least. What mattered was that the garage next door was wide open and his pickup was in it. The smaller house was a rental and vacation property. Sten kept it fully furnished, but he hadn't rented it to anyone since Madison had stayed there last spring.

Karin turned to her dad. "Do you have any idea why Liam's truck is parked in the garage next door?"

"I thought you knew," her dad replied. "Liam called Sten and Sten leased him the cottage."

Chapter Four

In the house, Coco ran to her room. The minute the little girl disappeared down the hall, Karin pitched her voice low and asked her dad, "Would you keep an eye on Coco? I'm just going over to talk to Liam for a minute."

"Kary." Otto spoke gently, like she was made of glass and about to shatter. "He's a great guy."

"Did I once say he wasn't?"

"Just give him a chance, that's all I'm suggesting."

"You're right. He's terrific and I intend to work with him and honor the importance of his place in our child's life. What more do you want from me, Dad?"

"Well, you could open your eyes. You're as bad as Sten was with Madison—pushing a good thing away for all you're worth."

"Not true." Yeah, Sten had been a thickheaded fool about Madison, ridiculously certain for way too long that it couldn't work out for them. But Sten and Madison were a completely different situation than Karin and Liam and her dad really ought to know that. "My eyes are wide open, I promise you."

"That man next door? He is not Bud."

As if she didn't know that—and she felt obligated, as always, to defend her dead husband. "Bud was a good man."

"Never said he wasn't."

The baby, whom she'd carried from the car in his baby seat, gave a questioning cry. "Shh, now. It's okay," she whispered to him. To her dad, she said, "I really can't have this conversation right now. I need to go next door. Will you keep an eye on Coco?"

Otto studied her face for several uncomfortable seconds before finally giving it up. "Sure."

"Thanks, Dad." She gave him a grateful smile and hustled to the baby's room as her newborn fussed in the seat. He quieted as soon as she wrapped him close in the baby sling Prim had given her for a shower gift.

At the cottage, she went in through the open garage door and was halfway up the interior stairs when Liam pulled open the door above that led into the laundry room.

"Hey." He beamed down at her like she was the one person in the whole world he'd been waiting to see. "Come on in." He stepped back and ushered her inside, leading the way to the kitchen that opened onto a deck with stairs down to the beach. The cottage had a similar footprint to the main house, with the entrance facing the hill behind it and the main living area looking out over the ocean.

Liam had all the kitchen cabinets open, with groceries piled on the counters. He gestured at the table by the slider. "Have a seat."

"No, thanks. I won't stay long." She stroked the curve of the baby's back. He wiggled a little, then settled against her.

"I like that sling thing. I need to get one." Liam stood too close, right there at the end of the counter with her—really, did he have to be so tall and broad and manly? "Keely has one," he said. "She uses it constantly. My niece Marie loves it."

"Liam. We need to talk about this." She tried to sound stern—but understanding, too.

He chuckled. "You sound like Mrs. Coolidge. Remember her, fourth grade? She'd get so disappointed if I didn't turn in my homework. *Liam*, she would say. *What am I going to do with you?*"

No way was she getting detoured down memory lane with him. That could be a very long trip. They'd known each other since the beginning of time, after all. "Moving in here, just out of the blue like this, is a little extreme, don't you think?"

"No, I don't think it's extreme in the least." He leaned back against the counter and folded his arms across that hard chest. He wore a lightweight blue sweater. The sleeves were pushed up, revealing forearms with just the right dusting of silky-looking hair and those sexy veins that only served to accentuate his gorgeous, hard muscles. "I'm really glad I thought of it. Lucky for me, it was empty. Sten says he took it off Airbnb and Vrbo because he's in LA most of the time. When he *is* here, well, Madison doesn't really want strangers right next door anyway. People can get intrusive, living next to a movie star—they're going to try to make it home during the holidays, did you know that?"

Karin rubbed the baby's back some more, soothing herself as much as her little boy. "Yeah, I knew that."

"The downstroke is that your brother said this cottage is mine for as long as I need it. He even gave me the go-ahead to fix it up any way I want, including a room for the baby. I'm thinking deep blue and a mural on the crib wall, like the one you did, except not. Maybe a dinosaur mural. Or stars and moons…"

She tried again to get through to him. "Liam, I just don't think it's a good idea, you living here. There are, well, boundaries, you know? We need to observe them."

"And I am observing them."

"No. You're moving in next door."

"Karin, come on. I'm in this house and you're in the other house. We definitely each have our own defined space. It's not like I'm suddenly asking to share a place with you."

"But I would rather that you—"

He cut her off. "Look, I know what our baby needs most now is you. But if I'm living here, he's going to know me as part of his life from the start. That matters to a kid and it matters to me. I can play backup parent from the beginning. Anytime you need help, I'm right next door." He pushed away from the counter and stepped in too close again. She steeled herself against all that charm and hotness. "This is a good thing, me being close by. You have to know that."

She backed away a step and tried another tack. "What about that beautiful house you built in Astoria?"

He gave an easy shrug. "It's too far away from my son. When I get around to it, I'll put it on the market."

"Just like that? But you *love* that house."

"My priorities have changed. But don't worry about it. I'm not selling it right away. If I suddenly decide I can't live without that house, it'll still be there. Right now, though, I need to live *here*, near you and the baby."

Oh, this man. Her heart could melt into a hot puddle of goo just listening to some of the things he said.

And that was the whole point, now wasn't it? *Not* to get a melted mush-ball of a heart just because a good man was trying to do the right thing by his child. She needed to stand strong on her own, be supportive of Liam as a coparent to their son, but remain mindful that he had his life and she had hers and having a baby together did not mean they *were* together.

"You're just going to do this, aren't you?" she demanded. "You're living in this house next door to *my* house no matter how I feel about it."

He took her by the shoulders, his big, warm hands so strong and steady, and he captured her gaze and held it. "You'll see. It's going to be great."

Back at the other house, her daughter greeted her at the front door. Coco had changed clothes. Now, her shorts were blue and her T-shirt was red. Yellow knit arm warmers covered her wrists to her elbows. She had a swatch of gold mesh fabric tied around her head and a red construction-paper star pinned to it in the exact center of her forehead.

"Wonder Woman, how's it going?"

Coco crossed her arms in front of her face. "Just tell me you need help, Mommy, and I will save you." Coco wiggled her eyebrows over the barrier of her arms.

"Whew." Karin made a show of wiping imaginary sweat from her forehead. "That is really good to know."

"I have lots of powers, Mommy." Oh, yes, she did. Coco had an iPad and she knew how to use it. She always did her research, superheroine-wise.

"What powers, exactly?"

"I have superhuman strength and I never get tired. I glide through the air on the wind. I have super speed and *agitally*. I can smell everything and see everything and hear the most smallest sounds."

"I feel safer already."

Coco stood tall. "You're *welcome*, Mommy." And off she flew toward the kitchen.

As for Karin, she went straight to her bedroom, pulled out her phone and called Sten.

He answered on the first ring. "How's my new nephew?"

"He's sweet and beautiful," she said loftily. "You're going to love him."

"I can't wait to meet him. Liam tells me you haven't settled on a name yet."

"No, we haven't—and about Liam…"

"Yeah?" The single word was freighted with challenge. She could just picture Sten drawing his shoulders back, standing a little taller. "What about him?"

Reminding herself that she would stay calm and not yell at her brother—for the sake of the innocent child sleeping next to her heart if for no other reason—Karin paced back and forth at the foot of the bed. "I am really upset with you," she said in a purposely soft, calm voice. "You could have at least discussed it with me before you leased him the cottage."

Sten snort-laughed. "And have you make up a thousand meaningless reasons why I shouldn't rent to him? No, thanks. He's family, Karin, in case you've forgotten. He's my brother-in-law and he wants to be near his kid. There's nothing wrong with that."

"I am actively resisting the powerful need to start shouting mean things at you."

"Go right ahead and shout. I can take it. Because I'm pissed at you, too. You have to give that man a chance, Karin. He wants to be there for your baby and it's part of your job to help him do that."

It was essentially the same thing their dad had said. It had aggravated her the first time she heard it. This time, it made her want to throw back her head and scream. She took a slow, deep breath before replying. "I *am* helping him, Sten. I support him totally as the baby's father."

"And yet you took forever to get around to telling him he was even going to be a dad. Karin, I really was starting to think you never would."

"Sten, okay." She stroked the baby's nearly bald head with one hand and pinched the bridge of her nose with the other because sometimes Sten gave her a headache—and because, yeah, he was right. "I messed that up, I admit it. But at least he knows now. He was there for his son's birth. And now, thanks to you, he's even living in the house next door."

"You're welcome."

She heard the humor in her brother's voice and couldn't help but smile. "I think Liam plans to be the most *involved* dad that has ever existed in the whole of time. And I think it's great, I really do. I am not getting in his way, I promise you. Liam will have every chance to be there for his kid."

"Good," said her brother. "That's how it should be. And now he's got the cottage, it will be so much easier for him to help you out whenever you need him."

"By that you mean you won't tell him that you've changed your mind and the cottage isn't available after all?"

"Way to go, little sister. I think you're finally getting the picture."

* * *

Karin did take her brother's words to heart.

She invited Liam over for dinner that night. He showed up right on time. When the baby cried, she let him do the comforting. A little later, for the first time, Liam changed his son's diaper—a loaded one, too.

Really, her baby's dad was one of the good guys.

And that was the problem. He was a good man and he wanted to do right and it would be oh, so easy to let herself believe that they could share more than a son.

She would just have to keep holding the line against any suggestion that the two of them should get married. Eventually, he'd come to see that her saying no had been the best thing for everyone involved.

Thursday after dinner, she asked her dad to watch the sleeping baby so that she could go over to the cottage and discuss DNA testing with Liam.

He answered the door looking way too handsome in black jeans and a dark sweater with the sleeves pushed up those amazing forearms. Really, it wasn't fair that he looked so good. She, on the other hand, wore the outfit she'd thrown on that morning—a stretched-out gray Henley-style tunic and yoga pants. She'd also run out of the house without bothering to check her hair or freshen her lip gloss.

Had she actually been naked with this gorgeous specimen of a man on four separate and glorious occasions? It seemed so very long ago…

And yet, it really had happened and she had the baby to prove it.

"Hey."

"Hey."

"Where's the baby?"

"Sleeping. My dad'll call if he needs me."

"Come on in." He gave her that smile of his, the magic one that could make a girl's panties combust, and led her to the sitting area.

She took a chair and got down to it. "I came to talk DNA. There's a lab right here in town. We can all three go together, you, me and the baby. Just name a date and time—or I can meet you there, if that works better for you."

"DNA?" He dropped to the sofa. "It's not necessary. I know the baby's mine. I don't need a DNA test and I don't care if we have one."

"*I* care, Liam."

His burnished brows drew together. "Don't do that."

"What?"

"Don't give me that look, Karin. Like you disapprove of me."

Now, she felt awful. "I didn't. I *don't*." She stuck her hands between her knees and leaned toward him across the coffee table. "Not at all. What I meant was, well, proof is so easy to get now. There's no reason *not* to get it. All it takes is a cheek swab and you'll never doubt that our little boy is yours."

He shook his head her. "I already have no doubts. I know you, Karin. You have absolute integrity. If there was a doubt, you would have told me so that day at Safeway." He spoke with total conviction.

Now, her cheeks felt too warm and her tummy all fluttery. "Thank you." Her throat had clutched. She gulped to loosen it up. "That was a beautiful thing to say to me."

He leaned forward, too, so earnest and determined. "I don't need a test, Karin."

"I hear you. But *I* do—and not because I have any doubt you're the baby's dad. It's just, I want that, for you to have objective proof. Even though I accept your word that you don't need it."

He dropped back against the cushions with a hard breath. "Sorry. I don't get it. But if it's what you want—"

"It is. Please."

The following Monday afternoon, together, they took the baby to a lab right there in town to have their cheeks swabbed. Liam, eager to use the new car seat he'd bought, did the driving.

Later, back at the Cove, mindful of her resolution to treat Liam with kindness and consideration, Karin invited him to dinner again. "About six, if you can make it."

He accepted with a wide grin and showed up an hour early. She refused to let herself get annoyed about that. Instead, she reminded herself that the guy planned to stay at the cottage indefinitely and she'd better get used to having him around.

Really, what was not to like about Liam? He was easygoing and also easy on the eyes. He even offered to help in the kitchen.

"I've got this. But you can help the kids with cleanup after if you insist."

He had a beer with her dad and jumped to his feet when the baby cried. "I'll get him." He headed for the bedrooms and she didn't stop him.

When it was time to eat, he carried the blue bundle with him to the dinner table, where Coco fawned all over him and the baby in his big arms.

Coco did have one complaint, though. "Liam. Mommy. Our baby needs a name. Nobody likes to be called just 'the baby.'" Coco wrinkled up her little nose in disapproval.

"He's a newborn," said Ben. "He doesn't know how to talk and he doesn't understand words. That means he has no idea what we're calling him."

Coco tossed her curly head. "Well, *I* care what we call him and I'm his big sister." She smiled sweetly and actually fluttered her eyelashes. "I will be happy to choose a name for him. How about Brecken? There's a boy named Brecken in my class. He talks without raising his hand and chews with his mouth open, but I still like his name. Or how about Kael or Ridge?"

Karin met Liam's gaze across the dinner table as he glanced up from the baby in his arms. His eyes gleamed with humor. The moment tugged at her heartstrings, somehow. She was reminded of the past, of their long history together.

When Karin and Liam were Coco's age, he'd had a big crush on their second-grade teacher, Miss Wu. One morning, he brought Miss Wu a handful of wilted wildflowers he must have picked on the way to school. At recess, a couple of the other boys had razzed him. They'd called him a kiss-ass. Liam had just laughed and walked away.

Karin, flanked by Prim and Naomi, had watched the exchange. She and her friends waited, wide-eyed, for the two bullies to follow him, taunt him some more, maybe even throw a punch or two.

Didn't happen. The boys just stared after him, looking baffled. Liam simply had that way about him, always had. A born charmer, so easy and comfortable in his own skin. Bullies never knew what to make of him.

Really, the only time Karin had seen the man at a loss was recently, in the first few days after he found out about the baby.

Across the table, Liam tipped his head to the side,

watching her. He offered, "My dad's name was George. Maybe George for a middle name?"

Coco piped up with, "I like Brecken better."

Otto stepped in. "Excellent suggestion, sweetheart. But I think your mom and Liam will be making this decision."

Coco released a gusty sigh. "Well, o-*kay*. I don't need to be the decider, I guess. Just as long as my baby brother gets a name."

Otto reached over and patted her shoulder as Karin asked Liam, "What do you think of Riley? Riley George Bravo?"

He bent to the baby and whispered something. Then, still leaning close, he turned his head as though listening for a reply. He straightened in his chair with a nod. "He likes it. Riley George, it is."

Tuesday around nine, after everyone had left the Cove but Karin and Riley, two of Liam's sisters knocked on her door. Harper and Hailey had come to fix up the baby's room over at the cottage.

Hailey said, "But we wanted to stop by, say hi to you and meet Riley first."

Karin invited them in and made them coffee. They took turns holding the baby and filling Karin in on their mutual dream, which involved hosting children's parties and producing community events at an old theater downtown. Both blue-eyed blondes, the sisters were less than a year apart in age. They'd gone off to OU together, majored in theater arts together and graduated together the year before. Now, they both lived in town.

"My new nephew is the cutest guy ever," declared Hailey when it was her turn to hold Riley.

Harper agreed. "He is adorable—and Liam is so happy. All he talks about is the baby."

Hailey asked, "Can you blame him? I mean, look at this little guy." She grinned at Karin. "Liam likes *you* a lot, too."

Karin wasn't sure how to respond to that—mostly because she was constantly reminding herself *not* to like Liam too much. "He's a really good guy." She tried not to wince at how lame that sounded.

Harper said, "Okay, maybe this is out of bounds…"

"But we're just gonna ask," Hailey picked up where her sister left off. "If you don't like the question, tell us to mind our own damn business."

"We won't be offended."

"Fair enough." Karin sipped her tea. She had a pretty good idea where this was going.

Harper scooted closer to the table and wrapped her hands around her coffee mug. "So…what's the story with you and Liam? We didn't even know you guys were a thing."

"Well, we weren't a thing, not really." Karin turned her teacup in a slow circle as she tried to decide how much to say.

"Riley here would beg to differ." Hailey bent close and nuzzled his fat cheek. "There must have been *some*-thing."

Karin confessed, "You're right. There was." It really had been terrific, her long-held secret fantasy come true—a few hot, stolen nights with the guy she'd crushed on so hard back in high school.

Harper reached over and gave her arm a reassuring squeeze. "Don't be sad."

Hailey looked concerned. "We didn't mean to upset you."

"You haven't. No way. It just, um, happened, between Liam and me. It started last December, on a girls' night out…"

She'd almost canceled on Naomi and Prim that night. Ben had come down with something and was running a low fever. She'd decided to stay home. But her dad and Sten had ganged up on her. She deserved a break, they said. Ben would be fine, they promised her. And she would only be a phone call away.

So she'd gone. "Believe me, with two kids and the Boatworks to run, I hadn't been getting a lot of nights out. My girls and I met up at Beach Street Brews. Liam just happened to be there that night, too, with some of his trucker buddies. He and I started talking. It was so easy between us. I couldn't get over that—then again, we've known each other all our lives, so why wouldn't we be comfortable with each other, right?" She met Harper's eyes and they shared a smile. "It was a great night. And so were the other nights we got together. But he wasn't looking for a relationship and neither was I. It was just for now and just for fun. And then, well, surprise, surprise. Riley came along."

Harper nodded. "It happens."

"Wedding bells, maybe?" Hailey asked, looking hopeful.

"No," Karin said gently. "He's an amazing guy and I like him a lot, always have." Maybe too much, but his sisters didn't need to know that. "We're not in love, though." It caused an ache in her heart to say it. But sometimes the truth hurt. She finished softly, "We just want the same thing and that's to do the best we can for Riley."

They left it at that. The sisters stayed for another half hour or so. Before they left for the cottage, Karin gave Hailey the blue teddy bear Liam had brought over that day Riley was born. "I want him to have it for the new room."

That Friday, the DNA results came through.

It was official. Liam was Riley's biological father.

That evening, Karin took Riley over to the cottage to talk to Liam about a parenting plan.

"Hey." He gave her his killer smile. "Come on in."

In the kitchen, he offered her something to drink. "I'm guessing no alcohol, with the nursing and all, but I've got juice and I picked up some of that raspberry tea you like."

"I'm good, thanks."

He let his gaze trail down to the baby, who was attached to the front of her as usual, lately. Karin kind of loved watching his face when he saw his son. His mouth got so soft and his eyes a little dreamy. It was too damn cute by half. "Mind if I hold him?"

She eased Riley out of the sling and handed him over. The baby blinked up at his father and then yawned.

Liam bent his head close and nuzzled Riley's button nose. "Lookin' good, RG." He glanced up and caught her watching him. "What?" But then, before she could answer, he gestured her forward. "First things first. Let me show you his room."

She followed him down the hall to the bedroom next to the master suite. It was all ready for Riley. "Wow. That was fast."

He looked up from whispering to the baby. "Yeah. I got right on it. Lots of online shopping with overnight shipping. I gave Keely a credit card and she ordered most of the blankets and baby clothes, all the baby supplies and a diaper bag. I picked out the furniture myself."

"It looks great." Open shelves over the changing table were stacked with everything a baby might need. The walls were dark blue.

"I love the teddy bears and the tree," she said of the wall mural behind the crib. One bear floated midway up the wall on a couple of heart-shaped pale blue balloons. Three others climbed the tree.

"Harper did that, the mural and the detail stuff. Hailey painted the walls blue. Then the two of them put the furniture where they thought it should go." He gazed at her steadily. "They mentioned you had them over for coffee."

"Yeah. It was great to see them. We had a nice little chat." *About you and me and why we're not getting married. But you don't need to know that, so please don't ask.*

He didn't. He was all about the baby as he circled the room, whispering things in Riley's ear, stopping by the easy chair next to the window and glancing up at Karin. "RG and me, we need to try out this chair."

"Go for it." She leaned in the doorway and folded her arms across her middle.

He sat down. "Check this out." He leaned back and the easy chair became a recliner. "Pretty sweet, huh?"

"Perfect." And it was. *He* was. Totally devoted to his surprise son. It brought her joy to see them together— joy and a bittersweet ache in her chest that Bud had never really been able or willing or whatever to show that kind of steady, doting love to Ben. At least with Coco, Bud had been more affectionate—when he was around.

"What?" Liam was watching her.

She waved the question away with a shrug.

He glanced down at the baby again. For a few minutes, they were quiet. Liam held Riley as Karin leaned in the doorway enjoying the sight of them, the feeling of peace that seemed to fill the blue room.

"He's sound asleep," Liam whispered as he rose. "I want to put him in his crib." It was all fixed up, with cute blue-and-white bedding, including soft bumpers to cushion and protect a newborn. The blue teddy bear was propped in a corner.

"Good idea," she whispered back.

He put the baby down and tucked the blanket around him, bending closer for another kiss.

Rising to his height again, he came to her. She pulled away from the doorway to face him.

And then he was taking her by the upper arms, his big hands so warm and gentle. He caught her gaze and held it, that beautiful smile flirting with the corners of his full mouth.

She just knew he would kiss her and that she would let him.

But he didn't. "Come on," he said. "You know you want that raspberry tea. I haven't taken the baby monitor out of the box yet, but I think we'll hear him if we just leave the door open."

Liam had one of those electric kettles. It heated the water in no time.

As she waited for the tea to steep, he pulled a Boundary Bay IPA from the fridge and popped the cap. "So, what's up?" His strong throat rippled as he took a long drink.

"I thought we should kind of get moving on our parenting plan."

With a slow smile, he shook his head. "Always with the plans."

They stood facing each other on the same side of the counter. She had a strong urge to whirl around, dart over to the table and pull out a chair, put some distance between them. If he came and sat down, too, the table would serve as a barrier to keep her from giving in to the longing inside her.

She felt he was always asking a certain question—he asked it with his eyes and his body language, with his very attentiveness. It was partly *will you marry me?* But it was more, too. He was asking for kisses. And slow, sweet caresses. He was asking for more nights like the ones last winter.

And maybe asking was too weak a word. Maybe he was more...anticipating. Waiting for the moment, the *right* moment to make his move.

What were they talking about?

Parenting plan. Right. "Structure is a good thing." Dear Lord. Could she sound any prissier?

He set his beer on the granite countertop and took a step closer. That brought him right up in her face. She should run for the table—or maybe right on out the door.

But she didn't want to run.

She wanted those kisses his eyes kept promising, wanted to just stand here and suck in the warm, delicious, manly scent of him, to admire the fullness of his lips and the chiseled perfection of his jaw, to drown in the baby blue perfection of those eyes.

"We really don't need a parenting plan, Karin."

"Uh." Her mind felt thick and slow. Warm molasses ran through her veins. "Yes, we do."

"RG is eleven days old. At this point, I just need to

be here whenever you want backup or a break. That's my job and we can't put that on a schedule. Not right now. Except when there's something at Bravo Trucking I have to handle ASAP, I'm yours. And RG's. Push comes to shove, you and our son are the priority and my business will just have to get in line."

What he said made perfect sense—not to mention making her feel looked-after, taken-care-of. It would be so very easy to give in, let him have his way about everything.

To let herself fall.

So easy, to love him, to give her heart and soul to him.

Easy and scary and not in her plans. Because it was better, safer, not to start counting on him. Not to let herself give her trust to him and take the chance that eventually he would let her down.

Her poor heart had had enough of that. She just couldn't go through that kind of hurt and disappointment again.

Good men got right behind the idea of stepping up and making a lifetime commitment when a woman needed them. But sometimes, in the long-term execution of that commitment, they started feeling trapped by the very thing they'd sworn they wanted.

Uh-uh. Not going there again.

Liam moved that extra inch closer. She could feel the warmth of him now, smell his clean, manly scent.

Really, he was much too close. She drew in a breath and her breasts met his chest. Her whole body tingled.

She ought to just step back. But she didn't.

He lifted a hand, slowly, the way a person does around a skittish animal, ready to back right off if she gave him the slightest indication she wouldn't welcome his touch.

She could not for the life of her give him that hint. The delicious anticipation was simply too great.

She thought of all the things a woman considers when she's just had a baby and a man looks at her as though he intends to kiss her.

If she ended up with her clothes off, how bad would she look to him? Her belly was too soft and her breasts were blue-veined and swollen, cradled in a nursing bra. Her panties? Plain cotton and not brand-new. How long had it been since she'd washed her hair?

And what did any of that matter?

There was no way she was getting naked with him tonight. She wouldn't get the go-ahead to have sex for weeks yet—not that there weren't a lot of other things short of the main event they could do if they wanted to.

Oh, why was she thinking about sex right now?

Why was she thinking about sex at all?

She wasn't having sex with Liam. Not tonight, not ever. He was her partner in parenting Riley and the last thing they needed was to muck up that important relationship with something as volatile as sex.

"You're blushing." He leaned close and whispered the words into her ear. His breath was so warm, tickling her earlobe and brushing the curve of her cheek. "You smell like heaven, Karin, always did. Now there's a baby lotion and a fresh-baked cookies sort of smell, too." He actually sniffed at her.

"Cookies? Excuse me?"

"Sorry. I smell what I smell and it smells really good." His lips were right there. She felt them, skimming, soft and warm, against her cheek. He nipped at her, gently, like she was an actual cookie and he wanted a taste.

The light pressure of his teeth on her skin made her gasp.

His hand touched her hair, those long fingers gently combing through it, easing out the tangled spots. He used to do that, stroke her hair, when they were in bed together. "I always loved your hair. Since way back when we were kids."

"You didn't." Her voice sounded so odd to her, husky and low.

"Yeah. It's dark as coffee, and shiny, with red glints in sunlight and a blue-black sheen to it by lamplight. And it's always kind of wild, falling every which way. Back when we were kids, I always wanted to stick my fingers in it, to pull on it and bury my face in it."

"I would've punched you out if you'd tried that."

"I kind of thought you might, so I kept my greedy paws to myself—and then in high school, those two dates we had?"

"Don't remind me."

"I wanted more with you, even then."

"Coulda fooled me."

"But we were barely eighteen, much too young to go being exclusive."

She laughed, a husky giggle of a sound that she quickly stifled. "I can't believe I'm standing here whispering with you, and giggling, too, like some brainless fool. I keep telling myself to step back, step away from you."

He nuzzled her cheek again. "How's that working out for you, Karin?"

"It's not."

"We've got a thing. You know we do."

"Riley is not a thing."

"Karin," he chided. "I'm not talking about RG."

"You *should* be talking about Riley. *We* should be concentrating on Riley."

His hand left her hair. He trailed a finger down the side of her throat, stirring up a naughty string of hot little shivers as he went. And then he put that finger under her chin to get her to look at him. His eyes burned into hers, the blue color deeper than usual.

"I've missed you," he said, "since you dumped me last March."

"I didn't dump you. How could I dump you? We weren't together."

"Yeah, we were. From that first night, I wasn't with anyone but you. How about you?"

"No. But you know what I mean. It wasn't serious. We weren't even dating."

"Karin."

"What?"

"Shut up." He stole a quick, perfect kiss. Her lips burned at the brief contact. She yearned, she really did. Every molecule in her body hungered for more.

And he knew it, too.

He knew it and he gave her exactly what she couldn't stop herself from wanting. Lowering his amazing mouth, he settled it more firmly over hers.

Chapter Five

Liam took care to kiss her slowly, with restraint and yet with promise. He knew she was right on the brink of breaking.

And she could break either way—in surrender. Or in flight.

He wanted her surrender, at least as much as he could get of surrender in a kiss.

"I'm not having sex with you," she said breathlessly against his mouth.

"I know." He'd read the damn books, after all.

Framing her boyish, beautiful face between his hands, he broke the kiss to gaze down at her. He'd always loved the way she looked, with those eyes that were blue and then green and then blue again, seeming to change colors in changing light. He admired those high cheekbones, that pointed little chin. And those plump, perfect lips that invited his kiss.

"It's just a kiss," he reminded her.

"Liam," she whispered. He heard longing in that whisper and he swooped in again to give her exactly what she longed for, going deeper this time, urging her to open, to let him in.

She resisted at first, but then, with a tiny groan, she gave it up. His tongue slipped between her softly parted lips and he tasted her fully as he let his hands wander a little, out along her slim shoulders, down her back.

Good. She felt so very good. She was making him ache, making him hurt in the best possible way.

He pulled her closer, pressing his hardness against her, cupping a hand at the back of her head to hold her in place so he could kiss her even more deeply. She was heaven in his arms and he had missed holding her, missed the fire between them, the way they bickered and nipped at each other.

It was really fun, with Karin. She was the girl he'd known forever, and yet the girl who kept changing. He'd lost her in high school because he'd told her right out that he didn't intend to be anyone's boyfriend. Then she'd married Bud Killigan, who was a couple of years older, a guy Liam hardly knew. And then last March, he'd lost her again, lost her before he even got a chance to persuade her she should spend more time with him.

He wouldn't lose her this time. Now they had RG and that made it necessary that they be together. One way or another, he would convince her she belonged with him.

Sometimes he got impatient. It was his nature to be so. But mostly, it didn't matter to him how long it took her to finally realize he was the one for her. Getting there definitely was half the fun.

With a sigh, she pulled away.

"Get back here," he commanded and dipped close to claim her lips again.

She only slid her hands up between them and pressed them flat to his chest, exerting undeniable pressure, the kind a man had no right to ignore. "I have to go, Liam." She gazed up at him, those blue-green eyes so serious. Her soft lips were red and swollen and he was on fire to taste them again.

That wasn't going to happen tonight, though. Reluctantly, he released her.

She stared up at him, looking earnest and adorable and turned on and embarrassed. "I shouldn't have kissed you."

He dared to put a finger against those perfect, swollen lips. "I'm glad you did."

"But we—"

"Karin."

She blew out a hard breath. "What?"

"It was a great kiss. Let it be." He pushed her mug and saucer toward her along the counter.

"Fine." She took the tea bag out of the mug, plopped it on the saucer and took a sip.

He heard a reedy cry from the baby's room.

She heard it, too, and set down the mug. "Time to go."

Could he get her to stay if he tried? Probably not. He'd pushed her enough for one night.

A few minutes later, in the baby's room at the main house, Karin nursed Riley and thought about Liam.

She really shouldn't have kissed him, but she couldn't quite bring herself to regret that she had. That kiss had been amazing. She refused to feel bad about it.

She just needed to make sure it didn't happen again.

That wouldn't be easy. Liam was proving to be a lot more persistent than she'd ever imagined.

Since the day he learned that she was having his baby, he'd gone right to work insinuating himself into every corner of her life. Her brother, her daughter and her dad had definitely fallen under the influence of Liam Bravo's charms.

Sten was all for the guy, lecturing Karin to treat him right, renting him the damn cottage without consulting her. Coco had what amounted to a kiddie crush on the man.

And since the day after Karin and Riley came home from the hospital, Otto and Liam had developed their very own private tradition: morning coffee, the two of them. Her dad would head over there at the crack of dawn. He'd stay for an hour or so and get back to the main house in time for breakfast.

When it wasn't raining, he and Liam would sit out on the mist-shrouded deck of the cottage together. Most mornings, Karin could hear them faintly, talking and laughing, like they were best buds or something.

Ben was the only one who held the line against Liam. Her older son was always polite around any grown-up. But he hadn't really warmed to Liam. He was civil around the baby's father and not much more.

Ben's reserve didn't stop Liam, though. He was always asking about Ben's latest science project and listening with rapt attention when he finally got Ben to open up a little about it. Twice already, he'd picked up Ben and a couple of teammates from soccer practice when Otto was stuck late at the Boatworks.

Okay, yeah. The more she thought it over, the more she came to the simple conclusion that Liam Bravo was amazing. He was amazing and she had a crush on him just like her daughter did.

But really, how long would he be living next door? When would he realize he missed his easy, independent single lifestyle?

Karin just needed to keep herself from counting on him too much. That way, when he finally agreed on a parenting plan and went back to his own life, she wouldn't be brokenhearted, wouldn't miss him too much.

She just needed to watch herself, not let herself start squabbling with him. Squabbling with Liam was far too much fun. And kisses? No more of those. And she really had to avoid any more trips down memory lane. They had far too much history and it made her feel way too fond of him to reminisce with him about stuff that had happened way back when.

No kisses. No reminiscing. No banter.

"I can do that," she said out loud to no one in particular—strongly enough to give Riley a scare. He popped off her breast and blinked up at her, startled.

"Oh, honey, it's okay…" Laughing softly, she guided him back to her nipple. "You've got a good dad and your mama loves you," she whispered to her baby son. "It's all going to work out just beautifully, you'll see."

As a rule, on Halloween, Karin or her dad would take the kids trick-or-treating along the streets above Sweetheart Cove. This year, Ben had declared himself old enough to take Coco without adult supervision and Karin had agreed to that.

But this year, it was raining. Steadily, in buckets. Coco whined all day and Ben looked grim and unhappy.

Around four, Liam showed up at the sliding door that opened onto the deck. Her dad let him in.

"Riley's sleeping," she said to Liam, when the two men joined her in the kitchen area where she was standing at the open fridge trying to decide what to whip up for dinner.

"No problem," Liam replied. "I'm not here to see the baby."

"We need to talk to you." Her dad shot a quick glance around the living area. "Are Coco and Ben still in their rooms?"

"Umm-hmm. I believe Coco is actively sulking because the rain very likely will mess up her Halloween. Ben's not happy about that either. He's focusing his frustration on working out issues with his latest science project, I think."

"As long as they're not in earshot, good." Her dad kept his voice low, just between the three of them. "We need to talk about tonight."

"There's a kids' Halloween party at The Valentine Bay Theater," Liam said. "There'll be games and some skits and a really simple haunted house—nothing too gory. And bags of treats for everyone."

Karin shut the fridge door and turned to face the men. "Right. I saw a flyer somewhere about that."

"It's a Hailey and Harper production, essentially," Liam explained. "Eight bucks a head to get in."

Otto said, "Liam and I were talking about it over coffee this morning, that it might be an option if the rain didn't stop. The kids could wear their costumes and do something a little different this year. Liam and I will take them and you can have the evening to yourself."

"We figured you might not want to take the baby out on a rainy night," added Liam. "And just as another option, if you'd prefer, I can watch RG and you can go with your dad and the kids."

She'd yet to get out her breast pump and she didn't really feel like dealing with that at the moment, anyway. Not to mention, Riley wasn't even two weeks old. She wasn't ready to be away from him for that long.

Liam read her so easily. "Too soon, huh?"

She nodded, though a Halloween party really would cheer the kids up. And to steal a couple of hours for herself?

Talk about a new mom's dream-come-true. "I have to admit, the idea of me and Riley and the second season of *Killing Eve*, that's pretty tempting."

"We thought so." Her dad seemed pleased.

"So we're on?" asked Liam.

She hesitated. Liam made it way too easy for her to say yes to him and his plans.

And come on. What in the world was wrong with that, when his plans inevitably involved ways to help her make life better for herself and her family?

"Thank you," she said to both of them. "I think it's a great idea."

Liam stayed for dinner—it only seemed right to feed the guy, what with him giving up his evening to take her kids out for Halloween.

They set off, the four of them, at a little before six, Coco dressed as Jewel the Dalmatian and Ben, in a light blue jacket and bow tie, as Bill Nye, the Science Guy.

Once they were gone, Karin grabbed a bottle of ginger beer and sat on the sofa. Sipping slowly, she listened to the steady drumming of the rain on the roof and thought that never in the history of women had there been such a perfect moment. Everybody gone except her baby, who was sleeping.

After she finished her pretend beer, she spent an hour on the phone catching up with Prim and Naomi. Then she made popcorn and watched three episodes of *Killing Eve*, only getting up to pee and to feed and change Riley when he cried.

It was after ten when the Science Guy, Jewel the Dalmatian and the two men arrived home. Of course, they'd stopped for ice cream after all the excitement of Harper and Hailey's Halloween extravaganza. Even Ben was jazzed up, sucking on a Starburst from his bag of treats and raving about the cool ways Liam's sisters had used dry ice to make fog.

"Mom. It was sick. That fog, it not only overflowed from the witch's cauldron. They had it pouring out of the mouth of a giant carved pumpkin and rising from the base of a gnarly 'hanging' tree."

Coco was so happy, she pranced in a circle. Her doggy ears bounced as she pawed the air, fake-growling when her grandpa suggested it was time to call it a night.

Otto insisted, though. "Kiss your mom good night and say thank you to Liam."

Ben and Coco dutifully pecked Karin on the cheek and offered up a duet of thank-yous to Liam. Then Otto herded both of them off down the hall to put on their pj's and brush their teeth.

That left Liam on the sofa with Riley in his arms and Karin standing by an easy chair trying to decide whether to sit down or start hinting that it was time for him to go.

He looked up from their son with a lazy, lopsided grin. "Don't worry. I won't stay long."

She couldn't stop herself. She grinned right back at

him and then said sincerely, "Thank you. You turned a big disappointment into a memorable event."

"For you. Anything." He said it quietly, kind of tenderly and yet teasingly, too, so that she could tell herself he was only kidding around.

She almost opened her mouth to remind him—teasingly, of course—that they were coparents, not a couple.

But why even say it, jokingly, or otherwise? He hadn't done anything to imply there was more than coparenting going on between them. Not really.

And he looked so relaxed and happy. He'd made her kids happy, too, and given her a precious evening all to herself. How could she keep her walls of emotional safety in place when he wouldn't stop being so damn wonderful?

He got up. "Walk me out?" Still holding the baby, he headed for the entry hall.

She followed along, far too content to be going wherever Liam led her. He turned and passed her the baby when they got to the door.

When she had Riley, though, Liam didn't step back. Uh-uh. He leaned even closer.

And she reminded herself to step back. But she didn't. Anticipation flaring inside her, she stayed right where she was.

Their lips met. Her heart lurched and then kicked into a deeper, hotter rhythm. She sighed against his parted lips.

"Thanksgiving," he said as he broke the tender contact.

Puzzled, and a little annoyed at how much she'd wanted that kiss to last longer, she frowned up at him over their sleeping baby. "Um. What about it?"

"We always have it at Daniel's."

Where was he going with this? "Okay...?"

That mouth she loved kissing way too much curled in a slow, ovulation-inducing smile. "This is an invitation, Karin. I want you and the kids and your dad to join me and the rest of the Bravos for our family Thanksgiving. Rumor has it that Sten and Madison just might be showing up, too."

"Do Daniel and Keely know you're inviting the whole Killigan-Larson crew?"

He did that thing, a lopsided grin coupled with a sexy glint in his sky blue eyes. "Say yes, and they will."

"That just doesn't seem right."

"What do you mean it's not right?" He had that look now, the patient one he gave her whenever she threatened to go off the rails over something he was trying to convince her to do.

"It doesn't seem right for you to just invite all of us without at least warning your brother and his wife first."

"It's a Bravo family thing. The more the better. We love a large group and our Thanksgivings and Christmases just keep getting bigger."

"But think about it. Now, counting Madison, there are nine of you again." A brother, Finn, had vanished years ago. The Bravos still had investigators looking for him.

"Karin." Liam spoke softly, gently, as though she were a not-too-bright child. "I know how many siblings I have."

"Of course you do, but I don't think you realize how many people you could potentially be talking about."

"Sure, I do."

"No. Liam, it could be a *lot* of people."

"Didn't I just say I know that and that it won't be a problem?"

"Think about it. Daniel, Matt, Aislinn and Madison are married, so you have to count their spouses."

"So?"

"So some of those spouses will probably have people *they* want to bring. And let's not forget your great-aunt Daffodil and great-uncle Percy. And Daniel's got three kids."

"Why are you telling me all this stuff I already know? Just FYI, Karin, it's *my* family."

She reminded herself not to raise her voice. She would wake the baby. "Well, I know that," she whispered.

"And guess what? Connor and Aly Santangelo got back together."

That gave her pause. The two had been married and then divorced years ago. "Seriously?"

He nodded. "They're in New York, but they hope to be back for the holidays. They remarried in Manhattan, a courthouse wedding a week and a half ago—the day after Riley was born, as a matter of fact."

"Which only further proves my point. Aly's got that big family of her own here in town. Will *they* all be coming? Liam, do you hear what I'm saying? Maybe there isn't room for four extra guests and a baby."

"It's Daniel's house, the family house. There's *always* room. And who all is coming is not your problem. All you have to say is yes. Just tell me you would love to come and bring the kids. I've already talked to your dad. He's all for it."

"You talked to my dad about it without even checking with me?" She spoke too loudly. Riley squirmed in her arms and let out a cry. She lifted him to her shoulder and rubbed his little back. "Shh," she whispered to him, "it's okay, Mommy's sorry she scared you." She rocked him side-to-side a little and he seemed to settle.

"Karin." Liam reached out.

"Don't." She stepped back to keep him from touching her. She wasn't sure why, exactly, she was so upset about this invitation. It just felt like…a big step. A step she wasn't in any way ready to take. A step she kept telling herself she would never take. "See, Liam. You have your family traditions and we have ours. So, doesn't it just make more sense for you to go ahead and go to your brother's the way you always do for Thanksgiving and we'll just have our family dinner here the way *we* always do."

"No." A muscle twitched in his square jaw. "That makes no sense to me at all. I asked you to come to Daniel's because *that's* what makes sense to me. I want you there, Karin. I want our baby there and your dad and Ben and Coco, too. And Madison and Sten, if they can make it up from LA. I want us all together. That's what Thanksgiving is, all the people you care about the most, together, if at all possible. And it *is* possible, completely possible, if you'll just say yes."

Riley started fussing again. She rubbed his little back, pressed her lips to his warm, silky forehead and said to Liam, "You're being purposely thickheaded."

"*You're* being pointlessly negative and obstinate."

"No, I'm just—"

"Enough." His voice was carefully bland. "Think about it, okay? Let me know what you decide." He pulled open the door and went through, shutting it behind him before she could say another word.

Chapter Six

A week went by during which Karin and Liam hardly spoke.

Early most mornings, she heard him laughing with her father out on the deck at the cottage. More than once, she saw him jogging along the sand in a hoodie and track pants, his shoulders so broad, his hips so lean and tight, his long strides carrying him quickly along the shoreline toward the rocks and shallow caves way down the beach. It caused an ache inside her just to watch him, to take in the sheer perfection of him.

Every evening when he returned from Bravo Trucking, he came to the house to visit his son. She would hand the baby over and walk away.

From the kitchen area or down the hall in her room or in the baby's room, she could hear him joking around with Coco and talking to Ben. He would give the baby to her dad when he was ready to leave.

One time, he was still in the great room with Riley in his arms when she wandered back out from her room to check on them. Her dad was nowhere in sight and the kids must've been in their rooms.

"Here's your mama," he said to his son and handed him over. "See you tomorrow, Karin." And he left her standing there by the slider. Turning toward the glass, she stared out at the dark sky. A moment later, she heard the front door open and then close.

Every time she saw Liam, she expected him to ask her if she'd made up her mind about Thanksgiving. She was *waiting* for him to ask, actually. And when he did, she would reply, *Thank you, but no.* She would say that she really had given his invitation serious thought and she appreciated it very much. However, thinking it over hadn't changed her answer; he should go to his family for Thanksgiving and she and her family would have their usual holiday dinner right here at Sweetheart Cove.

But the days went by and Liam didn't ask her, which made her feel edgy and uncomfortable inside her own skin. After all, she knew very well that he didn't *need* to ask again. The ball was in her court. She only had to give him her answer—and that was something she felt ridiculously reluctant to do until he brought it up.

Stalling much? Oh, yes, she was.

On Friday evening, Karin had Riley in the baby sling and had just finished cleaning up the kitchen after dinner when Liam tapped on the slider. She went over and let him in.

He glanced past her shoulder. "Otto okay?" Her dad was conked out, snoring in his favorite chair in front of the TV.

"Just tired. He had a long day rush-retrofitting a fishing boat. As usual, the owner wants the boat back in the water yesterday—sooner if possible."

Liam looked strangely wistful. "The kids?"

"Coco's got a birthday party sleepover. Ben's at a friend's, home at eight."

He came inside, bringing the scent of leather, moist night air and a hint of diesel fuel. "Kind of quiet without them."

"Except for the snoring and the WWE reruns, you mean." She shut the slider, extricated the baby from the sling and handed him over. "Here you go."

He got Riley settled on one arm and then held out a check.

She took it and saw it was made out to her. "Five hundred dollars? What for?"

"To help out with Riley. Since he's mostly with you at this point, I figure five hundred a month, for now. You need more?"

"Of course not." She had a terrible, hollow feeling in her belly as she realized he must be leaving, moving out of the cottage. Just as she'd expected, he was missing his big house and his no-strings lifestyle, so he was going to throw her some monthly child support and go back to his own life.

He spotted the cloth diaper she'd left on the back of a chair and grabbed it, laying it on one broad shoulder and lifting Riley against his chest. "Okay, Karin. Tell me what's the matter."

"Nothing," she lied.

"Then how come your face is red and your mouth's all pinched up?"

"I don't know what you're talking about."

"You're pissed off."

"No, I'm not." She folded her arms across her middle, realized how defensive the posture must look and made herself drop her hands to her sides. "So. When are you leaving?"

He whispered something to the baby and then frowned down at her. "Leaving?"

"Uh, well, I assume you're going back to your own place?"

"No. I live at the cottage now." He studied her, still frowning. "What gave you the idea I was moving out?"

She held up the check. "Well, I mean. I thought…" What *had* she thought? Now, she just felt foolish. "I don't know. I thought you were, um…"

"Paying you off because I won't be around?"

When he put it that way, it sounded awful—even though that was exactly what she'd thought. She waved the check again. "If you're next door, there's no need for this right now, is there?"

"What's my being next door got to do with paying my share of my son's living expenses?"

Nothing, she realized, and felt even more foolish.

He stroked the baby's head with his big hand. "I get it. The Larson-Killigan family is doing just fine. You're not hurting for cash and all the bills are getting paid."

"You'd best believe it."

"So open an account for him. Get going on his college fund. It's RG's money so save it for when he needs it."

Karin cast an uncomfortable glance at her snoring father. "Let's go talk in Riley's room."

"Sure." He followed her across the great room and down the hall.

She ushered him into the baby's room ahead of her. "Well," she said, after shutting the door. "I just thought we would get a parenting plan—you know, a legal, binding agreement. Whatever support arrangement we would make would happen then."

"Why go to court if we can come to an agreement without dragging the state of Oregon into it?"

It was a valid question. Damn it. "I don't know, I…" She blew out a hard breath and busted herself. "Okay, I'm sorry. I jumped to the conclusion that there was no need to start writing me checks unless you were moving out."

He seemed to relax, a ghost of a smile pulling at the edges of his too-tempting mouth. "Apology accepted—and I'm staying right here at the Cove. Get used to it."

The room was too small and he was too big and solid and masculine, standing there holding their baby in his strong arms, not quite smiling as he gazed down at her.

"Okay, then," she said, her voice aggressively cheerful, totally fake. "I'll leave you with Riley and, um, I'm right down the hall if you need me."

"That's good to know." He said it too softly, but with a slight edge of roughness that played a sexy, hungry tune on every nerve ending she had.

She pulled open the door and got out of there, fast.

That following Monday Karin went back to work on a part-time basis. Her plan was to go in for a few hours a day and take Riley with her.

But then when Liam showed up at the door Monday night and she mentioned that she was trying to catch up at the Boatworks, he offered to help out. "I can take Riley for you, at least a couple of times a week," he said.

"But what about Bravo Trucking?"

"It's great being the boss. I can pretty much set my own hours."

There was so much to catch up on. She could get a

lot more done without the baby there to interrupt her. "You sure?"

"Yeah. We should try it. See how it goes. How 'bout Wednesday, nine to noon, to start?"

It was too good an offer to pass up. "All right, then. You're on."

Two days later, she dropped Riley off at the cottage. Liam had everything he needed right there, all the baby paraphernalia a newborn could ever require. All she had to provide was enough pumped breast milk to keep Riley fed until noon.

She passed Liam the baby and set the bottles on the counter. "The milk can be out of the fridge for four hours. If you put it in the fridge, you want to bring it just to body temperature by running warm water over the bottle or letting it sit in warm water."

He kissed Riley's plump cheek and gave her a smug grin. "I've read all the books, Karin."

She bopped her forehead with the heel of her hand. "That's right. You're an expert."

"Yes, I am. Don't you worry. RG and me, we got it all figured out."

When she returned at noon, Liam handed her the sleeping baby.

"How was he?" she whispered.

"Perfect. I can take him Friday, same time?"

"You're on. Thank you." She started to turn for the stairs.

"Karin." Something in his voice sent a lovely shiver racing down her spine. She stopped and met his eyes again. "You don't have to thank me. I hope you know that."

She cradled Riley closer. It was cold out that day. "I, um, well, I appreciate all you do to help out."

"It's my job," he said and she knew he was going to say more. Stuff she probably didn't want to hear. Maybe he was finally going to ask her for her decision on Thanksgiving...

But then he only gave a slight shake of his golden head. "Go on back to the other house. It's cold out."

Relief and guilt swirling through her in equal measure, she turned and hurried down the stairs.

That Saturday night after the kids were in bed, Karin curled up in her room with a fast-paced thriller on her e-reader.

Her dad appeared and tapped on her open door. "Got a minute?"

"Sure." She set the device aside.

Otto just stood there in the doorway, looking at her. "Dad. What?"

He stuck his hands in the pockets of his ancient Carhartt work pants. He wore a plain white T-shirt and she found herself staring at his arms. They were strong arms from a lifetime of hard work, strong and scarred, freckled and dusted with reddish hair now gone mostly gray. Otto Larson was a good man, a man who had dedicated his life to taking care of his family.

"I'm just gonna say it, Kary. You need to give Liam Thanksgiving. He wants it, a lot. He's gotten himself all invested in this one simple thing, for our family and his family to celebrate Thanksgiving together."

"Dad—"

"I'm not finished. Liam's been nothing but here for you in every way that you'll let him be. Even if you can't give him all that he wants from you, you can say yes to Thanksgiving, you know you can."

"All that he wants from me? What does that even mean?"

Her father looked smug. "You really want to go there?"

She didn't. No way. "He sent *you* after me?" It came out sour and accusing. Because it was.

"No. He asked me what I thought of the idea and I said I was all for it. That was more than two weeks ago. He said he would ask you and then he didn't say anything more about it for days. So *I* asked *him* where we were on that. He said you were *thinking it over*. How long you planning on thinking about it before you actually give the poor man an answer?"

Her dad rarely annoyed her. But right now, he was definitely rattling her cage. "Liam Bravo is a long way from a 'poor man.'"

"Well, I for one feel sorry for the guy when it comes to you—and no. I'm not saying you should give him more than you're willing to give him. I'm saying it's Thanksgiving. And I know that *I'm* thankful for a man who is turning out to be a real dad to little Riley and who has knocked himself out to help you any way he can and been stepping right up for your other two children, too, showing an interest in who they are and what they're up to, driving them to and from wherever they need to go, even coming up with the perfect alternative when Halloween got rained out."

Everything her dad was saying?

True.

She pulled at a thread on the comforter. "You're right," she muttered reluctantly. "He's a terrific guy."

"So show him you appreciate all he's done. Say yes, we would love to go to Daniel Bravo's house for Thanksgiving."

When he put it like that, how could she say no? "Okay."

"What's that? Speak up."

"Fine, Dad. I'll accept Liam's invitation to Thanksgiving with the Bravos."

"Great. How 'bout doing that right now? All three kids are in bed and the lights are on over at the cottage."

Liam heard the tap on the slider and glanced that way. It was Karin, in flannel pajamas printed with penguins, a pair of Uggs and old Portland State hoodie with the hood pulled up over her hair.

"Got a minute?" she asked when he let her in.

He stared down at her upturned face, at that smart little mouth he couldn't wait to kiss again. "What do you need?"

She pushed the hood off her hair. "That Thanksgiving invitation still on the table?"

He felt a punch to his chest. The good kind, like his heart was reminding him that it was still beating. He could see her answer right there in those beautiful eyes. "You're saying yes?"

She nodded up at him, eyes bright and full of light, her face scrubbed clean of makeup, her dark hair a nimbus of shiny, wild curls. "We would love to come. All of us. You really think Daniel and Keely will be able to handle the crowd?"

"No problem."

"Well, okay, then. I'll, um, let you go…"

He caught her arm. "Just a second."

"Hmm?"

"This." He wrapped his other arm around her and swooped down to claim her lips.

She didn't resist.

On the contrary, she slid those pretty, slim, hard-working hands of hers up his chest and hooked them around his neck. "I didn't come here to kiss you," she said, as she kissed him.

He pulled her even closer. "Sometimes good things happen when you least expect them."

She laughed, her breath sweet with a hint of minty toothpaste, her body soft and warm in his arms.

He'd spent a lot of his life avoiding giving his heart. It was all due, he'd told himself, to the tragedies in his family when he was a kid—the disappearance of a brother, the sudden death of both parents. Loving people hurt so bad when you lost them and he loved too many people already. It was too late for him with his brothers and sisters, with Great-Uncle Percy and Great-Aunt Daffodil. He loved them before he learned the sad lesson that love ended up meaning loss that ripped you up inside.

But at least, his younger self had concluded, he could avoid the awful emotional danger of loving a woman.

His younger self hadn't known squat.

It took the birth of RG to show him the big picture. Karin had always been the one for him. All these years, he'd thought he'd dodged the love bullet. Wrong. He'd just been waiting for the right time to admit the truth to himself: Karin Larson Killigan owned his heart.

Sadly, Karin now seemed as determined as he used to be not to go there. He had a bad feeling that for her, the right time to give her heart to anyone was never.

She would probably mess him over royally. He'd get just what he'd always feared out of this deal: disappointment, hurt and the kind of loss that ripped a man's guts out.

He'd get everything he'd always been afraid of.

And he didn't even care. He wanted her and their baby. He wanted serious Ben, bubbly little Coco and stalwart, big-hearted Otto, too. He wanted to make a family with all of them, his deepest fears be damned.

If only he could find the way to get her to say yes to him.

"Liam." She sighed, her soft lips parting. He tasted her, nice and deep and slow.

Until she pulled back and her eyes fluttered open.

He touched her sweet, pointy chin, guided a wild curl behind the curve of her ear. *I want to marry you, Karin.* It sounded really good inside his head.

He almost went ahead and said it.

But he had a crappy feeling that laying another proposal on her right now would just ruin a great moment.

She'd given him Thanksgiving. He'd kissed her and she'd kissed him back.

For now, he would call it a win and not push his luck.

As it turned out, Sten and Madison couldn't make it home for Thanksgiving. Connor Bravo and his wife Aly didn't come either. They were still in New York, where Aly was training her successor at the advertising firm where she'd worked for the past seven years.

But even with two siblings and their spouses unavailable, Daniel and Keely's big house on Rhinehart Hill overflowed with family on Thanksgiving Day. The rest of the Bravo siblings came, including Matt with his wife, Sabra, and Aislinn with her husband, Jaxon, and also the housekeeper and foreman from Wild River Ranch where they lived. Keely's mom, Ingrid, and Keely's aunt, Gretchen, had arrived at the crack of dawn to help with cooking and general holiday prep. The food looked amazing. They had turkey, a gorgeous ham and a beautiful prime rib. And more sides than Karin could count.

Harper and Hailey, the family event planners, had set up ongoing games of turkey bowling and pin the feather on the turkey for anyone who wanted to play. They had a big pumpkin-shaped jar full of candy corn and made everyone guess how many candy kernels were inside for a possible prize of…a big bag of candy corn.

Daniel's twins, Frannie and Jake, were three now, happy kids who talked nonstop. Keely's baby, Marie, born the previous January, was already learning to walk. Marie staggered around on her fat little legs, constantly falling and dragging herself upright to try again. She was also a big talker, though her endless chatter made sense only to her.

Coco found Marie enchanting and spent a good portion of the afternoon holding the baby's fat little hand, helping her in her shaky efforts to stay on her feet. The attention delighted Marie to no end. She beamed up at Coco like she'd found a new best friend.

Ben took an interest in the twins. He bundled them up in their winter coats and took them out to the backyard for a long walk around the garden paths. The Bravo family basset hound, Maisey Fae, loped along in their wake.

Everyone made a big deal over Riley. Grace Bravo, the youngest of Liam's siblings, offered Karin her bedroom off the kitchen for a private place to nurse. Gracie suggested that Riley could have her bed if he dropped off to sleep—which he did, about a half hour or so before the big meal. Keely gave Karin a baby monitor to use and she surrounded Riley with pillows and left him to nap.

When they sat down to eat, Great-Uncle Percy and

Great-Aunt Daffy each gave a toast. Percy raised his glass to long life. Daffy, to true love. Aunt Gretchen said grace.

Karin, seated next to Liam at one of the two long pushed-together tables, felt his big, warm hand brush hers under the table as Gretchen recited her sweet prayer of thanks.

It was good, Karin thought, to catch up with the Bravos again. She'd put up a lot of resistance to coming here today. And now she found herself grateful that her dad had convinced her she needed to say yes to Liam's invitation.

As amens echoed around the packed table, she gave the man her hand, even opening her fingers a little, lacing them with his at his urging.

He leaned close. "I'm glad you're here."

She met those beautiful eyes and almost wished...

Well, better not even to let herself complete that thought. "Me, too," she replied. "I'm glad you invited us."

He gave her a smile that made the tall white candles in the middle of the table seem to burn even brighter. "So, you're having a good time?"

"I am. Very much so."

A teasing gleam made his eyes look even bluer. "Clearly, you should say yes to me more often."

Should she?

Doubtful. Coparents needed to respect each other's space. However, Liam Bravo was turning out to be a whole lot more than she'd ever bargained for. He was not only hot and tempting, but so persuasively persistent, as well. He was good to her kids and friends with her dad and thoroughly determined to do right by his child. She would be lying if she tried to tell herself she didn't find him extraordinarily attractive on a whole lot of levels.

He leaned a fraction closer. "What is that secretive smile you're giving me?"

"Just thinking that you're a really good dad." And he *was* a good dad, so she'd only told him the truth—only not all of the truth.

He laughed. "Do you give that look to all the good dads?"

And she went ahead and answered honestly. "Only you, Liam."

His thumb slipped in between their joined hands. He stroked her palm. It felt so good, so wonderfully thrilling and deliciously naughty.

And she was probably losing her mind a little what with all this…thankfulness she was feeling. Losing her mind and getting crazy ideas.

Ideas like how maybe she ought to be more open to him, to this attraction she felt for him.

Okay, yeah. She knew very well it would be better, smarter, not to mix their mutual parenting responsibilities with physical intimacy.

However, they were really good together in that way. They had chemistry, an excess of it. She'd always been drawn to him, since way back in high school. And the nights they'd shared at the first of the year still fueled her fantasies all these months and months later.

And now he lived right next door.

With every day that passed in which he was funny and kind and thoughtful, helpful and gentle and patient and so understanding—not to mention superhot—well, it just got harder and harder to remember that keeping a certain distance between them was key. It got harder and harder not to wonder why they shouldn't enjoy themselves a little.

As long as they both went into it with their eyes open, as long as they agreed that it didn't have to go anywhere, that they could be together just for now and just for fun. That if it didn't work out in the long run, they would act like adults, reestablish the boundaries and go on as Riley's parents who weren't together but wanted the best for their son.

Didn't divorced people do that all the time?

Really, if they kept it just between the two of them, didn't let the kids or her dad know, so that no one got unrealistic expectations of how things might turn out...

Well, she couldn't stop asking herself, what could it hurt?

Chapter Seven

The Larson-Killigan family had a tradition.

On the Saturday after Thanksgiving, they all went out together and chopped down their Christmas tree. They brought it home and stood it up in the picture window in the great room. From the attic, they hauled down box after box, each one packed full of Christmas decorations collected over the past three generations.

Then they all worked together decorating the tree, decking the fireplace mantel with boughs and twinkly lights and setting up the crèche that had belonged to Karin's mother's mother.

That morning, Liam appeared on the back deck just as Karin, Otto and the kids were sitting down to breakfast before heading to Oja's Christmas Tree Farm.

Karin glanced up and saw him standing there. She knew what was going on without having to ask, but she turned to her dad, anyway. "Looks like someone invited Liam."

"That's good!" enthused Coco. She bounced from her seat and darted over to the door, the black towel she wore for a cape flopping in her wake.

Otto swallowed a bite of pancake. "He has that Supercrew F-150. The console in front turns into a seat, so there's room in the cab for all of us and the long bed is perfect for hauling the tree home."

"Good thinking," Karin said wryly.

Coco, all in black to match her "cape," shoved the slider wide and threw out her arms to the sides. "Hi, Liam! I'm Raven. I have instant healing for me and for others. I travel to different dimensions. I teleport and *astro projet*—"

"She means 'astral project,'" Ben corrected.

Coco turned and glared at him. "You interrupted me. That's rude."

"Sorry," said Ben and crunched a bite of bacon. "But you might as well get it right."

Coco sighed, the sigh of all sisters put-upon by older brothers. "Now I can't 'member the rest—but come in, Liam. Have some pancakes. We got blueberry syrup and plenty of bacon."

Karin, who found she was not the least annoyed that her dad had invited Liam without consulting her, started to rise. "I'll get you a—"

"Don't get up." He was smiling at her, the smile she somehow felt was only for her. "I know where the plates and coffee mugs are."

"Well, all right." They shared a long look full of humor and promise and banked heat, one of those looks she decided she didn't need to think too deeply about. Not now, not on tree-decorating day.

It was good, what she felt for him. She might as well enjoy that goodness, whatever might or might not happen next.

Bottom line, she was getting used to having Liam in her day-to-day life. He wasn't going away and she could either accept the situation gracefully or grump around like a shrew trying to protect herself from some possible future heartache.

And yeah. Overthinking. She needed to cut that out, too.

Liam poured himself some coffee and carried his full mug and a place setting to the empty chair across from her. Karin pushed the platter of pancakes his way and he took four. Otto passed him the bacon.

Coco announced, "Here's the butter and the blueberry syrup for you, Liam."

"Thanks." He captured Karin's gaze again. Little zings of fizzy excitement went zipping all through her. "RG?"

"He went back to sleep after I fed him." She tipped her head at the baby monitor perched on the counter. "So far, not a peep."

"Eat up, folks," said Otto. "The tree farm opens at ten."

For once, the weather cooperated. It was cold out, but clear. They bundled up in winter gear and piled into Liam's big pickup. Otto and Ben sat in front with Liam. Karin sat in the middle in back, Riley in his car seat on one side and Coco in hers on the other.

At the farm, they wandered up and down the rows of trees, finally settling on a nine-foot noble fir with gorgeous, thick branches in majestic even tiers.

Back at the Cove, they took a break for hot chocolate

with miniature marshmallows. Then Karin cued up her holiday playlist. To the holiday stylings of Bette Midler and Michael Bublé, Weezer and NSync, they brought the tree in and stood it up in the tree stand. After that, they trooped up and down the stairs until every box of tinsel, lights and decorations was stacked in the great room, ready to roll.

Once they had the lights on the tree, they stopped for soup and sandwiches.

Karin was having a ball. She loved getting out all the old decorations, remembering who had made or bought or gifted the family each one, and when. They took turns holding Riley when he wasn't napping. Karin got out her phone and snapped lots of pictures. Liam did, too.

It was great, the perfect family activity, all of them working together to kick off another year of Christmas memories, the house all warm and cozy, full of holiday tunes and the smell of evergreen. Karin missed having Sten there, but Liam fit right in. Everything was perfect.

Or it was until they got around to setting up the crèche and Liam suggested, "The baby Jesus in the manger should be right in the middle, under the star."

And Ben piped up in his coolest, most dismissive Little Professor voice, "We like it a little to the side. And I don't think you even really need to be here, Liam. We've been doing this for years without you and we don't need you now."

Poor Liam, standing there with Riley on one arm and the manger with its glued-in hay bedding in his opposite hand, didn't seem to know what to say.

Otto stepped in. "Liam's here because I invited him," he said in a careful tone.

Ben chewed his lower lip. He looked miserable. Had he been this way all day?

Karin couldn't believe she hadn't noticed till now that her serious, levelheaded older son wasn't his usual agreeable self. She asked gently, "What's going on, Ben?"

He stuck his hands in the pockets of his tan jeans and hunched his thin shoulders. "Well, I just mean, we do Christmas with the family and he's not our family. He's not my dad or Coco's dad. He's just the baby's dad."

Apparently, that was too much for Coco. "Benjamin Killigan, you are not being nice."

Ben scowled at her, defiant at first. But then his face kind of crumpled. "Okay." He set down the star that fit into the steepled roof of the stable and turned to Liam. "I'm sorry. I shouldn't have said that stuff."

"Ben." Liam tried to reassure him. "It's all right."

"No, it's not. It's not all right. It's not all right at all." And he darted around Otto's easy chair and took off down the hall. They heard his bedroom door slam shut.

For a moment, no one spoke. There was just Bette Midler singing "Have a Yule that's cool..."

Liam glanced down at the baby asleep in his arms, and then back up at Karin. "Maybe I should go."

"No, you shouldn't." She held his gaze. "Please stay."

Her dad backed her up. "Yeah. Don't go. Your leaving won't solve anything."

For once, Coco had nothing to add. She stood by the sofa, blue eyes big and sad, glancing from one grown-up to the other as though hoping one of them would do what grown-ups are supposed to do and make it all better.

Karin suggested, "Why don't you guys go ahead and put the crèche together? I'll talk to Ben."

* * *

When Karin tapped on her older son's door, he didn't answer. She counted slowly to thirty before trying, "Ben?"

He responded then. "It's open."

She turned the knob and pushed the door inward. Ben sat on his bed hunched over his laptop, looking absolutely miserable and completely not-Ben. Her brilliant oldest child usually took things in stride and never lost his cool.

Karin asked, "May I come in?" She got a shrug for an answer and decided to consider it a yes. When she sat down beside him, the screen of the laptop showed he'd brought up his favorite video game, but hadn't started playing it.

He shut the laptop and set it aside. "What?"

She wrapped an arm around him. He stiffened at first, but then gave in and sagged against her. She dared to drop a kiss on the crown of his head. "I'm not sure where to start. Maybe if you told me what's bothering you?"

He tipped his head back. Their eyes met, but only for a moment. Then he looked down again. "I don't know, really," he muttered in the general direction of the floor. "I miss Uncle Sten. And now there's the baby. It's not Liam's fault, I know that. He's nice, but..." He made a frustrated sound in his throat. "Look. Everything's just different, okay? Everything's *not* the same." He looked up and their eyes met again. She smoothed his hair. It was one fussy, motherly caress too many. "Mom. Don't." He scooted out from under her arm.

Her heart ached as she let him go. Somehow, she managed to let several seconds of silence elapse before trying again. "Uncle Sten won't be gone forever."

He shot her a look of pure annoyance. "Two years. At least. Until Madison gets through making those movies she already signed up to make." Sten and Madison would settle right here in the Cove once Madison had honored her outstanding contracts. She said she was giving up acting, that she wanted a different kind of life—a family with Sten, a home in Valentine Bay.

"In the meantime, though," Karin reminded her unhappy son, "they'll be back whenever they can—including over Christmas. They both seem pretty sure they'll make it home during the holidays."

"Mom. I know that. And I just told you. It's not the same that they come back to visit. Like they're *guests* or something."

"I'm sorry, honey. It's just…the way life is. Stuff changes, you know? People move away. But the happy news is that, in Uncle Sten and Aunt Madison's case, they eventually will come back."

"I *know*, Mom. And I get that you want to make me feel better, but can you please quit telling me stuff I already know?"

"I'm just trying to find out exactly what has you upset, that's all. You mentioned the baby…"

He lifted one shoulder in a sort of half-hearted shrug, but that was all she got.

She suggested, "So the baby's just more stuff changing and that makes you feel unhappy?"

"Mom?"

"Hmm?"

"Can we just…not be doing this right now? Can I just go back out there and say sorry again to Liam and we can fix up the manger with the baby Jesus in the middle and just have a nice time finishing up the decorations?"

"Of course we can. But I do want you to know that

I'm here and ready to listen whenever you want to talk some more about this."

He dropped his head back and groaned at the ceiling. "Mom." He must have stretched that word into at least three syllables. "I *know*. Can we go back out now, please?"

She ought to just leave it at that. But she couldn't stop herself from taking one more stab at making things right for him. "I love you, Ben. I always have and I always will. Having another baby in the family can't change how much I love you or how much Uncle Sten loves you or your grandpa, either. We all love you so much. That's the one thing that is never going to change."

"I know, Mom." He said it kindly that time, with only a hint of exasperation. "I love you, too."

They returned to the great room, where Ben went straight to Liam. "I really am sorry for what I said."

"Apology accepted," Liam answered in that easy way he had. "And you know, I think you're right about baby Jesus. A little to the side is better than directly under the star."

At ten that night, Liam was in the office he'd set up at the cottage. With RG to consider, he wasn't spending as much time at Bravo Trucking as he used to. Having a baby meant rearranging priorities and being more flexible.

He could get a lot done from home, he'd discovered, working at night when RG was with Karin. He liked to watch the fuel situation closely, change his buying strategy whenever better options presented themselves. And he kept on top of the shippers and the brokers he used. Trucking was a cash flow intensive business. If people started paying late, he needed to know and either stop dealing with them or make sure they started paying timely again.

The doorbell rang just as he was thinking he would call it a night.

What do you know? It was Karin—in blue pajamas dotted with snowflakes this time and a green hoodie. Same Uggs as before.

"Is it too late?" she asked.

"For you?" He couldn't stop himself from grinning. "Never."

She held up her phone. "My dad will call if Riley wakes up."

"You should have just brought him over."

"No." She raked the hoodie off her head, revealing all those untamed curls he loved. "It's always best to let sleeping babies lie."

Liam stepped back and ushered her in. "You want a drink or something?" he offered as he shut the door.

She shook her head. And then she took a step forward.

And then, without him having to do anything but open his arms, she was flush against him, all sweet warmth and perfect softness. She surged up. Her mouth met his and clung.

God. She tasted good. He could kiss her forever. No woman had ever felt as right as she did in his arms.

She dropped back to her heels, breaking the kiss, but letting him hold her. "I've been telling myself that we should…." The words petered out. She frowned up at him, her cheeks pink, her breath coming fast. "I don't know how to say this."

"Sure you do." He bent and brushed a kiss between her eyebrows. "Take your time."

"Could we maybe sit down?" She seemed nervous. It

was cute. Like they were back in high school again and she wasn't quite sure how to act with a guy.

He took her hand and led her toward the main room. In the sitting area, he turned on the gas fire and pulled her over to sit beside him on the couch. She set her phone on the coffee table. "Okay. It's like this. I was thinking that maybe you and I could kind of see where this thing might go between us."

Satisfaction filled him. At last they were getting somewhere. He couldn't resist pressing the point a little. "So you're finally admitting that we had a thing—that we *are* a thing?"

She groaned and covered her face with her hands. "Okay. Let's not get caught up in the *thing* controversy again."

"Just admit it's there, between you and me, and I'll let it go."

She dropped her hands, squared her shoulders and drew in a slow breath. "Then yes, okay? It's definitely *there*, between us."

"It never went away."

She pursed up those way-too-kissable lips. "Is this you letting it go?"

He touched her hair—and she didn't duck away. Taking total advantage of this perfect moment in which she was finally saying at least part of what he wanted to hear, he guided a wild curl behind the shell of her ear. "So maybe I want to rub it in a little. Sue me."

She poked him in the side with an elbow. "You're just asking for it, mister."

"You bet I am."

She laughed. And then she sighed. Her cheeks were bright pink. He found her irresistible like this, all shy and kind of awkward. "I was, um, thinking, hoping that we could just have it be between you and me, not say anything to the kids or my dad."

He didn't want to be her secret. He'd *never* wanted to be that. And he especially didn't want to be her secret anymore. But he also didn't want to blow this chance with her. "*Yet*, you mean. Not say anything to anyone *yet*."

"Yes, Liam. I mean, you know, see where it goes."

That didn't sound so bad—scratch that. It sounded damn good. For now, anyway. "Agreed." He took her by the shoulders and pulled her close.

She let him, even tucked her dark head under his chin. They sat quietly, staring into the fire. He stroked her hair some more, kissed the crown of her head and breathed in the citrusy scent of her shampoo. She shifted and let out a sigh.

"What?"

"Nothing." The way she said it, he knew there was definitely something.

"You worried about Ben?"

She didn't answer immediately, but when she did, she told the truth. "Yeah, a little. I think he feels kind of left out. Coco's such a charmer. Her heart is wide open. She's never had a problem demanding what she needs. Ben's the serious one and sometimes he kind of fades into the background. Now there's another boy in the family. Ben's no longer the only son."

Liam stroked a hand down her arm. It felt so good, just to sit here, the two of them, touching. Talking. "And then there's the baby's dad who isn't *his* dad, a guy who moved in next door and is always butting in on all the family events."

"Ben loved the Halloween party," she reminded him.

"And he seemed to have a great time at Daniel's on Thanksgiving."

"But then I kind of pushed my luck with baby Jesus, huh?"

She chuckled, the sound both sweet and rueful. "Ben does think you're a good guy, though. He's said so more than once." She tipped her head back and met his eyes. Hers were sea-blue in the firelight, and troubled. "The truth is, Ben didn't really have a great relationship with Bud—I don't mean Bud was abusive or anything. He was a good man, but kind of hard to talk to. He was gone a lot, working. And when he came home, he was distant and distracted. There were money problems. Plus, Bud hardly knew his own dad. His parents got divorced when he was only two and Bud stayed with his mom, and then she died when he was just nineteen. He didn't seem to know where to start trying to be a dad himself. He was better with Coco, but with Ben he just kind of wasn't *there*."

It was a lot, what she was telling him. More than she'd ever said about her husband before. Liam knew he had no right to resent the guy, but he did. For causing Karin pain and making her wary of trying again—because no matter how she tried to be fair to her husband's memory, it was pretty damn clear that Ben, Sr. had not been around as much as he should have.

In a weird, twisted and unacceptably selfish way, Liam resented that Karin had married the other guy in the first place. If she'd only waited until he got his head out of his own ass, he would have had a lot easier time convincing her she belonged with him.

But then, if she'd waited, there would've been no Ben and no Coco. And the more he got to know Karin's kids, the less he could picture a world without them in it.

She pulled away from him and sat up. "I guess that was way more information than you ever needed."

"Get back here." He caught her arm, but gentled his hold—and his attitude. "Please?"

"I did love Bud." She met his gaze, defiant. "But it was young love, you know?"

He didn't, not really. Releasing her arm, he trailed his fingers over the worn, soft fabric of her sleeve until he captured her hand. "The kind you grow out of?" He turned her hand over and bent close to kiss the heart of it.

"The kind that isn't strong enough to weather the rough patches."

He tugged on her fingers until she swayed toward him again. Gathering her in, he tipped up her chin and took her mouth. She opened for him and he sank into the kiss, drawing it out, making it last.

When he finally lifted his head, he eased both hands under her hair, lacing his fingers at the nape of her neck, tipping her face up to him with slow strokes of his thumbs. "I want to ask Ben if he'll come with me to Bravo Trucking. I was thinking tomorrow, just him and me, a drive up to Warrenton in the afternoon."

"You're looking for my permission?"

"I am, yeah."

"What if he turns you down?"

"That's okay. I'm not gonna pressure him. If he says no, I'll say it's an open invitation. If he changes his mind, he just needs to let me know and we'll make it happen."

She dipped her chin in a nod. "It's all right with me—but be prepared for Coco to want to come, too."

"I was more thinking a one-on-one with Ben."

"I get it. Just giving you a heads-up."

He didn't want Coco feeling left out. "I'll take her, too. Just her and me, another time."

"That actually might pacify her. But are you sure you want to be driving my kids back and forth to Warrenton to take the Bravo Trucking tour?"

"I'm sure." He kissed her again. Because she tasted so good and she'd admitted she wanted him. It wasn't enough, what she was offering, to be together, but only in secret. Not nearly enough.

But it was a start.

And from now on, he needed to have his hands and his mouth on her every chance he got.

That kiss led to another. And another after that. He actually had her hoodie unzipped before she called a halt.

"I need to get back." She zipped up again. "Morning comes early when you've got three kids."

"Damn," he said with a smile. "For a minute there, I thought I was about to get lucky."

"You are." She leaned close and caught his earlobe between her teeth. At his groan, she laughed. "Just not tonight."

He asked only half-teasingly, "Do you have your doctor's approval to fool around with me?"

"I will. My checkup's on Monday." She bunched up his shirt in her fist and yanked him close for another smoking kiss. "And this time we're using two forms of birth control."

"I've got the condoms."

"Great. And after Riley was born, I got an implant before I left the hospital."

"Taking no chances, huh?"

"That's right." She kissed him again, but pulled away much too soon. "You'd better come over for breakfast.

You can talk to Ben then. I'll help you out with Coco, say I need her at home to get going on the Christmas baking."

"Works for me." He yanked her close again and covered her mouth with his. For a moment, she gave in and let him hold her.

But only a moment. "I mean it." She grabbed her phone. "I need to go home."

Reluctantly, he followed her to the door.

The next morning, as usual, Otto came by the cottage for coffee.

Liam mentioned that he hoped to take Ben up to Warrenton that day to show him around Bravo Trucking.

"Kissing up to my grandson, huh?"

"You'd better believe it."

"You'll make Coco jealous."

"Coco will get an invite of her own."

Otto set his mug down on the table and stared out the slider. It was raining pretty hard, the sound a steady drumming on the roof and the deck. "Is that what Karin needed to talk to you about last night—you taking the kids to Warrenton?"

Liam shook his head. "The tour of Bravo Trucking was my idea."

Otto gave him a long, considering look. "So what *did* my daughter want to talk to you about last night?"

Liam got up, got the coffeepot and refilled their mugs. "Lots of things," he replied, mindful of his promise to Karin that they'd keep their new togetherness just between the two of them for now. "We've got a kid. There's all kinds of stuff we need to deal with, day to day."

Otto Larson was nobody's fool. His mouth curved in a secret smile. "You're saying you'll need to spend time, just the two of you, on a regular basis to discuss RG's care, is that what you're telling me?"

"Pretty much."

Otto stared out the window some more. Dawn was slowly breaking, revealing a gray, overcast sky. "She had a rough time, with Bud—and don't get me wrong. Bud wasn't a bad guy. Just too young, wanting to do the right thing and yet not quite up to the job. You'd better be good to her."

"I'm trying, Otto."

"I know, son. I like that about you."

At breakfast, Liam made his move. "I need to head to Bravo Trucking today for a couple of hours. Ben, would you like to ride along with me?"

Ben looked up from his scrambled eggs. His eyes were wary. "What for?"

"Thought you might get a kick out of a tour of the place." He sent a quick smile in Karin's direction, but didn't let his gaze linger. She looked way too damn pretty in a flannel shirt with her hair escaping every which way from the messy bun she'd put it in. "I already cleared it with your mom."

Karin confirmed that. "Fine with me if you want to go."

"Could be fun." Liam kept his tone offhand. "Check out a diesel engine, maybe go for a ride in a semitruck."

Those serious brown eyes flashed with interest, but Ben played it cool. "Okay, I'll go."

"Good. We'll leave in an hour or so, maybe grab a burger on the way back?"

"Sure. I'll be ready."

Coco had somehow managed to restrain herself till then. But she was not the kind of girl to let a good time pass her by. "'Scuse me, Liam? *I* like trucks. Can I please go with you guys?"

"Not today, honey." Karin eased in gracefully with her interference play. "I really need your help with the Christmas cookies."

"But what about Ben? He always helps, too. We should all help because helping is good."

"I kind of want to see that engine," Ben ruefully confessed.

Karin suggested, "I'm also going to need help next weekend with the fudge and divinity and candy cane bark."

Liam trotted out his perfect solution. "How 'bout this? Ben and I will go this week. Coco, I'll take you with me next week. You can each see the trucks and help your mom with the candy and cookies, too."

"All right!" Coco agreed, beaming. "I like making cookies and I like trucks, too!"

The baby monitor on the counter came to life with a questioning cry. The table quieted. They all knew the drill by then—it was always possible that RG would fuss for a minute and then go back to sleep.

Not this time, though. His cries grew more insistent.

Liam glanced at Karin, who was already looking at him. "Please do," she said with a grin and a wave of her hand.

He pushed back his chair and headed for the baby's room.

The rain had let up by the time Liam and Ben got on the road to Bravo Trucking. It was a little awkward, with just the two of them. They hadn't spent much time alone together up till then and Ben's outburst the day before kind of hung in the cab between them.

Liam cued up a playlist on low, just to have a little noise in the background. He asked about soccer. Ben's team, the Valentine Bay Velociraptors, had just wrapped up their fall season. The boy answered Liam's questions as briefly as possible. The subject of soccer died a quick death.

Next, Liam tried science. Ben said he was working on a special project, studying the temperate rain forest of the Pacific Northwest, which stretched from California to British Columbia and was the largest temperate rain forest on the planet. The science conversation fared better than sports, lasting a good ten minutes.

After that, Liam let the playlist make the noise for a while. It wasn't too bad.

Ben really perked up when they got to Bravo Trucking. He happily trotted along beside Liam, who took him through the corporate office, the fuel island and the shop. Even on a Sunday, Liam had a couple of things he needed to deal with in his office, but the few truckers hanging around the driver's lounge were happy to keep Ben busy, telling him stories of the road, answering his every question.

Liam took him out to get an up close and personal look at that diesel engine as promised, and to get a quick rundown on the different types of trailers—from dry vans, to refrigerated trailers, to flatbeds, step deck trailers and lowboy trailers used to haul freight. And for the big finish, Liam took him for a ride in a Kenworth W900B, the kind he used to drive when he first started out hauling timber for Valentine Logging.

It was way past noon when they headed for home. Ben had more questions about the trucking business and the conversation flowed naturally, Liam thought. Halfway there, he pulled the pickup in at a little roadside diner. It was nothing fancy, just burgers, fries and milkshakes. There was a small, fake Christmas tree by the door strung with tinsel garland, lights and shiny balls. The sound system played Christmas tunes.

They got a booth in the back corner and a waitress brought their food. Liam was trying to come up with a good way to maybe get Ben talking about the baby Jesus incident the day before. But he had nothing, really. Every time he came up with a possible opener, he cringed before he could get the words out.

So what, exactly, was on your mind yesterday when you ran for your room?

Maybe not.

Or *Do you resent having me around, Ben? Can we talk about that?*

Yeah. No. Maybe something less direct: *How's it working out for you, having a new baby brother in the house?*

Ugh. Somehow every conversation starter he considered sounded like lame psychobabble in his head. He had no clue where to begin.

And Ben was suddenly way too quiet again. They stuffed fries in their mouths and sucked down their milkshakes, avoiding eye contact as much as possible.

Then Ben surprised him.

The kid ate a giant bite of his burger and stared directly across the booth at Liam as he chewed and swallowed. "I kind of want to ask you something," he said when his mouth was finally empty. "It's got nothing to do with trucks."

Liam resisted a sudden urge to squirm in his seat. "Go for it."

Ben dropped his half-eaten burger to his plate and slurped up more milkshake, setting the tall plastic glass down with a definite clunk. "Well, Liam. I mean, you're always so nice. It makes me nervous. What's up with you?"

Chapter Eight

Liam had to hand it to the kid. "Way to go, Ben. We might end up having a real conversation, after all." Ben frowned at him. Liam ate a french fry. "Define 'nice.'"

"Hmm." Ben took a moment for another giant bite of his burger. Then he said, "You're just too great about everything. You never get mad and so far, you're always there when my mom needs you. You think Riley is the best thing ever, even when he's pooping his diaper and screaming. And you never seem to get annoyed at Coco—I mean, I love my sister but sometimes when she won't stop talking it's like…" He put his hands to either side of his head and made an exploding sound. "And what about you and Grandpa?"

"I like your grandpa."

"Exactly. You and Grandpa are like best friends all of a sudden. You get along with everybody. It's like you actually believe there's a Santa Claus—big news,

Liam. There isn't. Santa is physically impossible and as an adult, you should know that."

"Ben."

"What?"

"I do know there's no Santa Claus. I've known for years and years."

"I didn't say that I think you *believe* in Santa Claus, I said you *act* like you do."

"Point taken. I just felt the need to clarify."

"Liam. Are you messing with me?"

He busted to it. "Yeah. Maybe a little."

"I thought so. And it's okay—but that reminds me. Coco still believes in Santa, so you better not ruin it for her."

"Coco will never hear the truth about Santa from me. I promise you that."

Ben pointed a french fry at him. "Make sure you keep that promise."

"I will—what else makes you nervous about me?"

Ben devoured that fry and two more. "You're always around."

"You sound kind of pissed about that."

"Not pissed, not exactly."

"Then what?" Liam asked. Ben just looked at him, frowning. Liam let the wordless moment stretch out as Bing Crosby warbled "Do You Hear What I Hear?" from the speaker in the corner above their booth.

Ben shook his head. "I don't know. But I'm not pissed at you, okay?"

"Got it. So, you say I'm always around..."

"Because you are."

Liam shrugged and reminded him, "Your grandpa is always around."

Ben gave him that look, the one that said, *grown-ups are so dense*. "Well, yeah. Grandpa lives with us."

"And I live next door. Your brother is my child. It's a good thing, the right thing, for me to be around a lot. Plus, I *like* being around a lot."

Ben stared at him long and hard. "Do you really?"

"Yeah. I do. Really."

"Well, my dad was hardly ever around." Ben said that too softly, his gaze shifting downward. He said to his plate, "I hardly even knew him. And I don't think he liked me very much."

Pay dirt.

And now Liam was scared to death he would blow it. But he'd signed on for this, so he waded in anyway. "I would bet Bravo Trucking that your dad did love you, Ben."

Ben shot him a sharp glance, then went back to examining the puddle of ketchup on his plate. "You're just saying that because that's what you're supposed to say about a kid's dad."

"Uh-uh. You're the kind of kid any dad would be proud of. You're smart and you put other people first, which believe me, *I* didn't when I was your age. You look after your sister and your mom and your grandpa and RG, too. I've only known you for six weeks and I love you already."

Ben snort-laughed. "Right." But at least he looked up and met Liam's eyes.

"It's true, Ben. I really do love you. A lot." Liam realized how much he meant those words as he said them. He also felt so damn sorry for Bud Killigan. For Bud, it was too late to show his own son anything ever again—and Ben was watching him across the table, brown eyes steady.

Liam forged ahead. "It's also true that I didn't know your dad, but I do know that sometimes grown-ups can get so wrapped up in their own problems that they don't realize they're not giving the right signals to the ones they love."

"Signals?"

"Yeah. I mean, sometimes people fail to show how much they love the ones who matter to them, they get lost in the things that are bothering them. When that happens, they can miss their chance to show their love to the ones who mean the most to them. I would bet that's what happened with your dad."

Ben got that look. Like he was deconstructing his latest science project. "You mean that my dad's dead and how he really felt is not provable, so why not just tell myself he loved me?"

"I meant what I said, Ben. Your father loved you. Maybe he didn't do the best job of showing it, but that doesn't mean the love wasn't there."

"But it's not *provable*." Ben tapped a fist on the table for emphasis.

"So what? It's a hell of a lot more likely that he did than he didn't—and come on, what did I just say? Who *doesn't* love you? Everybody I know loves you."

Ben's mouth twitched, as though he was trying not to grin. "You're exaggerating."

"Nope. Truth. That's all you'll ever hear from me."

Ben grabbed his milkshake and sucked down the rest of it in silence—until the end, the part kids always loved most. Noisily, he sucked air. "I'm done." He set down the red plastic glass. "Thanks for the lunch."

"You're welcome."

"We should probably get back on the road."

Liam debated whether he should try to keep the man-to-man moment going. But he didn't want to mess with whatever progress he'd made.

He grabbed the check. "All right then. Let's go."

Things were quiet in the pickup as they headed home. Liam didn't fill the silence with music this time. A little quiet never hurt. And maybe Ben would have more to say.

They were five miles from Sweetheart Cove, when Ben asked, "So you're staying, then? You're not going away?"

"I'm staying." His own voice sounded so sure and he wondered, was he promising more than he could deliver?

No. However it worked out with him and Karin, he meant to be there—and not only for RG. "There's nowhere else I would rather be than with you and your mom and RG and Coco."

"And Grandpa." Ben said it more as a reminder than a question.

"And with your grandpa, too."

Karin rang Liam's doorbell at nine that night.

He opened the door and then just stood there, grinning at her. "God, you're good-lookin'." She wore yoga pants and a giant Welcome to Valentine Bay sweatshirt, her hair in a bun, same as that morning, untamed curls escaping every which way. "No other woman could ever compare."

She put one foot behind her and executed an actual curtsy. "And as you can see, I got dressed up real fancy."

"I've always been a big fan of the natural look."

"Oh, I'll just bet you have." She held up her phone.

"No telling how long I'll be here. Riley was kind of fussy today."

"You'd better get in here, then." He took her arm, pulled her inside with him, shut the door and reeled her in close. She melted against him. For several perfect minutes, there was just her mouth and his mouth, the feel of her body pressing close to his, the glide of her eager hands up over his chest and around his neck.

Too soon, she broke away and grabbed his hand. "Come on. We need to talk." And she led him into the main room, turned on the fire, pushed him down on the sofa and sat on his lap.

There was more kissing. On his lap like that, she was rubbing him right where it mattered most. He considered all the things that would be okay for him to do to her without her doctor's approval. There were a lot, now that he thought about it, and all of them tempted him.

But then she pulled away again and slid off his lap to sit next to him. She leaned her head on his shoulder. "So. How'd it go today with Ben?"

"Great. He got a tour of the yard, hung out in the driver's lounge. We went for a ride in one of the trucks. I think he had a good time."

"You, um, get a chance to talk to him?"

He balked. Suddenly it seemed wrong to tell her what her son had said over burgers and fries. "We talked, yeah."

"And?"

He rubbed the back of his neck, stalling. "It turned out to be kind of a man-to-man thing."

"That's good, right?"

"What I'm trying to say is I'm not sure I should betray his confidence, you know?"

She got that look women get, a little angry, a lot superior. "One, he's nine years old. Two, I am his mother. Three, that I am his mother means I need to know what's bothering him. And four, did he ask you not to tell me what he said to you?"

"No, he didn't. It's just…" He sought the right words. They didn't come, so he settled on, "Karin, some things a kid doesn't want to tell his mother."

"He's *nine*," she insisted, those beautiful eyes pleading now. "Just tell me this much. Did he mention his dad?"

Her begging eyes did him in. Screw the bro code. He couldn't keep stonewalling her. "Yeah. Ben said he didn't think his dad liked him."

"That's not true." Frantic color flooded her cheeks.

"Hey." He put up both hands in complete surrender. "I believe you. We argued over it. I tried to get him to see that his dad could love him and not be any good at showing it."

Her pretty mouth trembled. "Do you think you convinced him?"

"Not a clue. But he didn't seem upset, honestly. Just kind of puzzled at the weirdness of adults."

"Yeah. He's like that. My little professor…" Her eyes were fond and dreamy—but then she glanced at Liam and demanded, "What else did he say?"

"He wanted to know if I was going to stick around. I told him that I wasn't going anywhere."

She gave him a slow nod, but her eyes spoke of doubts. "It's better not to make him that kind of a promise."

He disagreed. "It's a promise I intend to keep."

"Liam. You never know how things will turn out. People think they want one thing and then, as time goes by, they realize they want something else altogether."

"I know what I want. And I told Ben the truth. I live here and I'm not leaving."

She bit the corner of her lip. "Look. I think you just need to know something. When I married Bud, I was pregnant with Ben." She stared at him, apprehensive, as if she expected him to be surprised.

He wasn't. Not in the least. "I kind of figured as much. People do that, you know?"

She scoffed. "Get pregnant accidentally or get married because they're pregnant?"

"Both."

"Well, we *were* in love, Bud and me."

"Yeah. You told me that last night."

"Bud swore he was all in—with me, with the baby. He made a lot of promises. I was young and hopeful and crazy about him. I just knew we were going to be happy together forever and ever. I said yes. We got married…" Her voice faded off. She stared into the middle distance, her eyes far away.

And then she said, "It was mostly downhill from there. Before Ben was even born, Bud had turned angry. Distant. I think he came to realize that what he really loved was life on a boat. He wanted his freedom. I just wanted it to work with us. I wanted it so much.

"For a while after Ben was born, Bud seemed…better, I guess. He even said that he wanted another baby. Looking back, I think he was trying to get behind being a husband and a dad. At the time, I was just ecstatic. I thought we were going to be all right. So we had Coco. And things were okay, for a while. But it didn't last. Finally, on that final night he was home before he died, we had a big fight. He said he wanted a divorce and I said that was just fine with me. I meant it, too. I knew we were done, that what I'd believed was lasting love just…wasn't. We never should have gotten married in the first place. A week later, the salmon troller he was on sank in the Bering Sea."

Liam reached out to her slowly. She'd always seemed so strong to him. Not now, though. Right now, she was fragile as glass. "I'm sorry. So sorry, Karin. For Bud. And for you."

She flinched when he touched her cheek. But then, with a shuddery little sigh, she sagged against him. "I hate that he died. I hate that he didn't have time to… I don't know. Get to know his kids? Figure things out? Find a little happiness, a life that really worked for him."

"Yeah." He pressed his cheek to her hair and wished he had something helpful to say. "People shouldn't be allowed to die until they're at least eighty and they've worked through all their crap and made peace with their loved ones."

She tipped her head up and looked at him, her eyes wet with unshed tears. "Exactly. There oughta be a law."

On the table, her phone lit up and vibrated.

She pulled free of Liam's hold and grabbed it. "Hey, Dad." Liam heard Otto's voice faintly on the other end. "He's probably just hungry. I'll be right there." She hung up. "Gotta go."

Liam wasn't ready for her to leave yet. She needed time, after the tough things she'd said to him. Time for him to hold her and kiss her some more, time for him to ease her fears, to reassure her that things with Ben really were going to be all right. He wished he could just go over to the main house with her, help her with the baby, sleep in the same bed with her.

But already she was pulling her shell of self-reliance back around her. She'd learned all the wrong lessons from her troubled marriage and her husband's sudden death.

Liam considered himself an upbeat guy. He looked on the bright side as much as possible.

But when it came to Karin, sometimes he wondered if he would ever really break through.

Ten minutes later, Karin sat in the comfy chair in Riley's room with her feet up on the fat ottoman and Riley at her breast. She rubbed his velvety cheek with a finger and whispered, "I love you, Riley George. I love you so much..."

She let her head fall back against the cushion and closed her eyes.

Raw. She felt raw and too open, after the things she'd told Liam tonight. It had seemed best, to explain it all, give him the whole truth about poor Bud. He needed to understand why she wasn't willing to give in and give the two of them a real shot.

Why getting serious with him was out of the question.

Liam was such a good guy and surprisingly persistent.

But she needed to keep a realistic perspective on their situation. No way was she letting herself get in too deep with him. He kept saying he wasn't ever leaving, that he wanted to be with her and her family. She was sure he meant it.

But just because he meant it now didn't mean he wouldn't change his mind someday.

She simply couldn't take that risk. Giving herself to him and then losing him, having him look at her the way Bud used to, like he wondered how he'd got himself into this mess—well, that could break her. And she couldn't afford to be broken. She had a family to think about.

After tonight, she was definitely reevaluating her brilliant plan to climb into bed with him again.

Uh-uh. He would be far too easy to fall in love with. Having a secret sexual relationship with him was just begging for trouble.

No. The sex thing couldn't happen. She needed to make it clear to him she'd changed her mind about that.

Liam got up early Monday morning and drove to Portland for some meetings at the office there. He didn't get back to the Cove until seven that night.

After a shower and some takeout he'd picked up from his favorite Italian place in town, he called Karin. She didn't pick up. He debated just heading over there, saying hi to Otto and the kids and getting her promise that she would be over as soon as she got everyone settled for the night.

But their thing was a secret thing. He wasn't supposed to do anything that might clue the family in to what was going on between them.

So he left a message. "I miss you. Come over as soon as you get the kids to bed?"

And then he went to his home office and dealt with email and messages, feeling antsy, distracted and so damn eager to have her with him again.

Finally, at a quarter after nine, the doorbell rang. He raced to the front hall and yanked the door wide, planning to sweep her up in his arms and kiss her hard and long.

The tortured look on her face stopped him cold. "What?"

"I'm sorry," she said. "But I never should have suggested that you and I get something going again."

He gaped at her. "Wait. No. What are you talking about?"

"I'm talking about you and me. Liam, you know it's a bad idea."

"I don't know any such thing."

"Well, you *should* know. Because it *is* a bad idea." She wore a sweater over jeans and a knit shirt. But it was cold out, with a brisk wind. She was shivering, her arms wrapped around her middle, her hair wilder than ever, the wind catching it and blowing the dark curls along her cheek, across her forehead.

"You're freezing." He stepped back and gestured toward the main room. "Just come in. I'll turn on the fire, fix you some of that tea you like. We'll talk this out."

"No."

"Karin—"

"I really can't. I don't know what I was thinking when I suggested we should start in with each other again."

"Look. You're freaking out. It's okay. We can talk about it—just talk, that's all."

"No, Liam. Talking won't change anything."

"You're shivering." He reached for her.

She stepped back before he could touch her. "No. Really. I just wanted to tell you, to let you know where we are on this. We need to focus on Riley, not end up in bed together. Having sex again, you and me, it's not a smart idea and it's not going to happen."

Five minutes ago, he couldn't wait to see her face. Now he just wanted to put his fist through a wall. He had a thousand reasons why she was all wrong about this. He wanted to start spouting them, frantically, one after the other, until he'd changed her mind.

But where was that gonna go? Nowhere. He could tell by the tilt of her head and the set of her mouth that she wasn't going to give him an inch.

So be it. If she didn't want to be with him, screw it. He was done with this noise.

"Well, okay then," he said. "I can take Riley for a few hours Wednesday and Friday, in the morning, same as last week."

"Liam, please don't be—"

"You've made your point, okay? No need to pound it into the ground."

He watched her throat move as she swallowed. A dark curl caught on her lip. She swiped it away. "All right."

"Wednesday. Nine in the morning. I can do eight, if that's better."

"No. Nine is great. Thanks."

"Don't thank me. He's my kid. Good night, Karin." He shut the door.

Chapter Nine

Karin went home hating herself a little, and yet certain she'd done the best thing for her, for Liam, for Riley. And for Ben and Coco, too. None of them needed Karin and Liam to get into something together and then have it all go to hell. For kids, especially, consistency mattered. Romantic drama between the adults they counted on could scar them for life.

Tuesday morning, Otto went over to the cottage first thing, as usual. When he came back, he didn't say a word about what was or wasn't going on with her and Liam. But he had that look. Like Karin had kicked a puppy or something.

She felt like such a complete jerk.

And it only got worse.

Early that afternoon, she was sitting in the little breakroom at the Boatworks eating a tuna sandwich with Riley snoozing in his carrier on the chair beside her. He made a small sound in his sleep, sort of a cross between a sigh and a gurgle. She glanced down at him.

And she realized that he looked just like Liam—a baby Liam with fat cheeks and no hair. Riley was going to break a lot of hearts, no doubt about it.

Something happened in her chest, like a pinch and a burn. She ached. For Liam. She wanted...

To talk to Liam. To tell him that their baby looked just like him. She wanted to whisper with him, to laugh with him. She wanted to sit next to him in front of the fire.

She wanted so many things, none of which she was ever going to get. Loving a man entailed risk. And after Bud, she was definitely risk averse.

Plus, Liam was sick and tired of her crap. She didn't blame him, she truly didn't. He probably wouldn't want anything to do with her now, not even if she begged him on hands and knees.

And her dad was still giving her dirty looks.

That night, once all three kids were in bed, she went and stood by her dad's recliner and demanded, "Did Liam say something to you about me?"

He muted the TV and then pointed the remote at her. "Liam didn't say a word to me about you. Not one word."

"Then why do you keep looking at me like you're pissed off at me?"

"Because something's bothering Liam and something is way off with you. My guess is, you two are having problems. And I know Liam well enough now to be reasonably certain he'd do just about anything for you. And that means *he's* not the one at fault."

"First of all, we aren't together, Liam and me. How can we have problems?"

"That's a question you need to answer for yourself."

"And second, you're *my* dad. You're supposed to be on *my* side, and yet you jump right to blaming me."

He grunted. "It's not blame, not really. It's more that I'm frustrated with you."

"Oh, really?"

"Yeah, Kary. Really."

"I'll bet you're not *frustrated* with Liam, now are you?"

Her dad heaved a weary sigh. "I'm so proud of you, Kary. I always have been, and even more so in the last few years. It was awful, what happened with Bud. But you've never been one to whine about how rough you have it. You work hard at the Boatworks. You're an amazing mother and you've created a good life for the kids and for yourself, too."

"Thanks," she said flatly.

"It's only the truth."

"And I know you, Dad. I know what you're doing here. Just hit me with the rest of it."

"All right." He swiped a scarred hand back through his thinning hair and leveled his faded blue eyes on her. "Truthfully, Kary, when you know you've messed up and you don't want to admit it, you're a brat, pure and simple." He pointed the remote at the TV and the sound came back on.

She just stood there, glaring at the side of his head, waiting for him at least to glance her way again. He didn't. "I take it I'm dismissed?"

"I love you, Kary," he muttered, still not looking at her. "I love you and you need to work things out with Liam and that's all I have to say on the subject." He stared at the rerun of *Two and a Half Men* as though he hadn't already seen it ten times before.

Karin fumed. She longed to go full-out drama queen

on him right then. But what good would that do—except to prove him right?

Head high and mouth shut, she whirled for her room, where she closed the door, sat on the bed and called Naomi. "My dad's pissed at me and I really can't blame him," she confessed.

"Hold on," said her lifelong friend. "I need quiet for this." A minute later, Karin heard a door shut on Naomi's end. "There. Silence. Such a rare and beautiful thing."

"Naomi, I messed everything up."

"Let me guess. This is about your hot baby daddy, right?"

"Don't call him that. He's so much more than that—and I hate that you know me so well."

"No, you don't, you love it. What happened?"

"Riley looks just like him."

"Kary. Kids do have a tendency to look like their parents."

Whipping a tissue out of the box on the night table, Karin swiped at her suddenly leaking eyes. "My dad called me a brat and I think he might be right."

"Oh, baby. Pretend that I'm hugging you and tell me everything."

That took several minutes and three more tissues.

"So then," said Naomi. "You want to be with Liam, but you're *afraid* to be with Liam."

"Yeah. Completely. On both counts. I want another chance but I still don't want to rush anything. I still want it to be just between him and me, at least for a while, because I have no idea what I'm doing and what if it all goes to hell? That wouldn't be good for anyone, especially my children—oh, and what does it matter what I want, anyway? I've screwed everything up with him six ways to Sunday. He'd be crazy to give me another chance. *I* don't even like me very much right now."

"Well, *I* love you."

Karin fell back across the bed and sniffled at the ceiling. "I love you, too. You're the best, Naomi."

"And what are you going to do now?"

"Try again, anyway?" Karin answered with a little moan.

"That's the way you do it—except minus the question mark. You need to be owning that stuff."

"I'm going to try again, anyway. Period."

"Yeah! Go get him, tiger."

Easier said than done.

Wednesday, she put on her best jeans and a red sweater and took ten whole minutes fiddling with her hair and putting on blusher, lip gloss and mascara before she took Riley to Liam's for the morning.

The extra effort got her nowhere.

Liam hardly even looked at her. "Hey, RG." He reached for Riley.

She handed him over, along with an insulated pack full of bottles of frozen pumped milk.

"Great," he said, and hooked the bag over his big shoulder.

She'd planned to ask him for another chance, she really had. But her throat locked up and the words wouldn't come.

"Noon?" he asked, stroking Riley's back, his blue gaze locked on his son.

"Uh, yeah. Noon is good."

"All right then." And he stepped back and shut the door.

It was the same at noon. She rang the bell and Liam

answered with Riley all ready to go. He passed her the baby, confirmed the time she would be dropping him off on Friday—and shut the door.

That night, Prim called. Naomi had told her everything and Prim wanted to know how she was doing. Karin explained her complete failure to get Liam to so much as look directly at her. "Let alone give me a chance to try to reach out."

Prim gave her a pep talk and she hung up sure she would do better on Friday.

Didn't happen. The baby handoff was faster, if possible, than it had been on Wednesday. She found herself standing alone on the step, minus the baby, staring at his shut door. At noon, he passed her Riley—and closed the door. Again.

Her dad got home at two that day to hang the outdoor lights on the porch, the back deck and down the outside stair railings, front and back. An hour later, Karin was straightening up the great room when she glanced out the slider and saw her dad and Liam hanging the lights together.

At four, when the kids got home from school, the men were over at the cottage putting up outdoor lights there, too. She knew because Coco and Ben had stopped over there before showing up at the main house to beg Karin to be allowed to go help.

"We already asked Grandpa and Liam," pleaded Coco.

"It's okay with them if it's okay with you," said Ben.

Karin gave her permission. The two ran out the slider and didn't come back.

By quarter of six, she had dinner all ready. The outside lights looked great. Karin turned on the tree lights and the star in the crèche and the lights on the mantel, too. She bundled Riley up and took him with her to see how the work was going.

They'd finished hanging the lights on the cottage, too. The big, multicolored bulbs lined the eaves, the railings and the stairs, so cheery and festive, pushing back the cold, foggy night. Feeling unsure and way too nervous, she mounted the steps to the deck.

They were all there, inside, in the living area, decorating a tree that stood near the wide picture window. For a long, bittersweet moment, she hung back in the shadows, cradling her baby close, just watching. They already had the lights on. Liam stood on a ladder holding a big, lighted star. He slipped it over the top branch, took a moment to prop it up nice and straight and climbed back down. The kids and her dad were busy hanging ornaments. Nobody had spotted her out there in the darkness, not with every light on inside.

Really, she didn't want to interrupt them. They seemed to be having such a great time. Dinner could wait.

She started to turn—and then stopped herself.

Even if Liam had decided she wasn't worth the trouble relationship-wise, they still had a baby to raise. He got along with her family and he really didn't seem to be going anywhere.

Sneaking around out in the dark, avoiding him, was no way to behave.

Riley made a tender little cooing sound in her ear as she marched to the slider and knocked on it.

"It's Mommy!" Coco's gleeful cry was clear even through the glass. She hung the ornament in her hand and ran to shove the slider wide. "Come in! We are decorating Liam's tree."

"I see that. It's looking good." She cast an admiring

glance at the tree—and her gaze collided with Liam's. Collided and held.

She pasted on a smile. "Just wanted to see if anyone was hungry?"

"We're *starving*," moaned Coco.

Karin was still staring at Liam as he stared right back at her. She suggested, "Why don't you all come on back to the house, have a quick dinner and then you can finish Liam's tree?"

"Good idea," said Otto. He turned for the pile of coats tossed on one of the chairs and handed the top one to Ben. Coco ran over there and grabbed hers.

Liam didn't move.

"I hope you'll come, too." Karin's stomach was all twisted in knots. Riley, picking up her anxiety, had begun to squirm in her arms. "Please."

Liam didn't smile. But his mouth got…softer. And his eyes got deeper somehow. "How could I say no?"

Dinner lasted maybe twenty minutes, max. They shoveled down the stew she'd made and everybody pitched in to make short work of cleaning up.

They were all pulling on their coats again as Karin finished wiping the kitchen counters.

"You coming?" asked Liam. She glanced up from the sponge in her hand as he pulled on his jacket. His eyes were ocean blue, beckoning her down to drowning. "Please." He said it so softly. Just for her.

And she felt…hope, like a bright pulse of sheer happiness, lighting her up inside.

"Yeah," she said. "I'll grab some cookies and the baby and be right over."

Three hours later, Liam's tree was fully decorated. They all agreed that it looked fantastic. Karin plated the cookies she and Coco had baked and Liam made hot chocolate—with marshmallows—after which he produced a deck of cards and challenged them all to a game of slapjack.

They played for an hour or so. By then, both kids were yawning.

Otto said, "Come on, you two. Time to go home and get ready for bed."

Coco whined, "Not yet…"

Ben tried bargaining. "Just one more game."

Karin shook her head. "Your grandpa's right. It's getting late."

The kids gave it up and grabbed their coats.

Trying for offhand and not really succeeding, Karin said, "I was thinking I would just hang around here with Liam until Riley wakes up." She'd fed him an hour ago and put him in his crib there at the cottage.

"Great idea." Liam gave her a look that sent a sweet shiver up the backs of her knees.

Her dad tried really hard not to smirk. "Come on, Ben. Coco. Kiss your mom good night and let's go."

As soon as her dad and the kids were gone, Karin sat on the sofa and tried to figure out what to say first. Liam, who'd carried the last of the empty cocoa mugs over to the sink, returned and sat beside her.

She felt the cushion shift, but couldn't quite bring herself to look directly at him. Not yet. The great room was suddenly very quiet. Because, sheesh. Where to even begin?

She stared at the tree and considered remarking on the beauty of it. But they'd pretty much covered that subject before the kids left.

Cautiously, she turned her head toward the man beside her.

He was looking right at her, a knowing grin tugging at the corners of that mouth she might actually get to kiss again, after all—maybe even tonight. "You got something to say to me?"

The butterflies in her stomach went wild, bouncing around in there, fluttering madly. "So much for my dad not figuring out what's going on between us."

"Not much gets by your dad. I like that about Otto." He continued to gaze at her, his eyes low and lazy, like a big, golden timber wolf contemplating his next easy meal. "And did you just admit that there *is* something going on between us, after all?"

She wished he would just grab her and kiss her and they could skip the part where she confessed her own stark terror of this dangerous magic that sizzled between them. "I freaked out, okay? I freaked out and then when you said I was freaking out, I lied and denied it. I'm sorry, Liam. I'm such a coward. I don't want to get hurt again. I don't want my children hurt again. I want to protect myself. But I want to be with you, too. I want it so much."

"Hey." He said it gently and her heart just melted. "I understand. It's okay. And Karin, I would never hurt you."

"I know you wouldn't, not on purpose. And you've been amazing, you really have, with me, with my kids and my dad. And our son is so lucky to have you, Liam. A lucky, lucky little boy."

He reached for her then, slowly, giving her plenty of opportunity to duck away. She didn't. He framed her face between his hands. "I'm not going to hurt you, Karin. I mean that. I just want to be with you."

"Me, too. I do want to be with you." Gladness pulsed through her, simply to feel his touch again. "But I still…" Her chest felt so tight, bursting with emotions that terrified her at the same time as they filled her with hope and yearning. "Just you and me, huh? Nobody else has to know until we see how it goes."

He shook his head. "Didn't you just say that your dad's already on to us?"

"He'll leave it alone if we make it clear we want it that way."

"Fair enough. Not a word to anyone, Otto included."

"Not even in the morning when he comes over here under cover of darkness and you two drink coffee and talk about…whatever you talk about."

"Manly things."

"Oh, I'll just bet."

"I won't talk about you with him, Karin, not even then. Not until you're ready."

"Thank you," she whispered. He smelled so good, of soap and evergreen and the wind off the ocean at night.

Slowly, he brushed his lips across her mouth, back and forth, setting off sparks, making her ache in the best kind of way. The light caress sent a hot pulse of desire straight to her core.

He eased his fingers back into her hair, combing them through it. "I'm so glad you're here. I hope RG sleeps for hours." He fisted her hair, pulling it a little the way he'd said he'd always wanted to do back when they were kids.

She teased, "Good luck with Riley sleeping for hours…"

"You're right." Liam caught her lower lip between his teeth and bit down with a growl. "We need to get moving here. He could wake up at any time." Slowly, cradling her face in his hands, pulling her with him, kissing her all the way, he stood. Once they were both upright, he pulled her even closer.

They shared another kiss. A deep one that went on forever, until her whole body quivered in eagerness and a pleading groan rose in her throat.

"Time for bed." He took her by the waist and flung her over his shoulder, like a fireman saving her from a burning building.

She would have cried out in mock protest, but the last thing she wanted to do was take a chance of waking the baby, so she settled for playfully kicking and pounding his broad back as he carried her off down the hall.

In the master bedroom, he shut the door, took her to the king-size bed and let her down to the rug—but he didn't let her go. He ran both hands down her arms and then back up over her shoulders. His touch felt so right. He cradled her face again and kissed her some more.

When he lifted his head that time, she gave the room a quick once-over. "The bedroom looks great." It was in grays and tans, with black-and-white prints on the walls.

"Thanks. Let's get naked."

She laughed. "Eager, much?"

"How did you guess?" He plucked at the sleeve of her sweater. "This is in my way."

She grinned up at him. "I got my checkup."

"Yeah?" Oh, those eyes of his. He could make her come with just a look.

"I officially have the all clear to do naughty things with you." She sounded breathless. He made her that way.

"Good." He took the sweater by the hem. "Arms up." She obeyed his command and he swept it up and away.

She frowned at him. "Wait a minute. You shut the door. We won't be able to hear—"

"Yeah, we will—stay right there." He went to the dresser and grabbed the baby monitor she hadn't noticed until then. "I have two receivers, one for out in the living area and this one." He flipped it on. The small screen showed the crib and Riley asleep in it. "Infrared, so I can see him even when the light's off. Cool, huh?" He set it on the nightstand.

"Very cool—but do you have condoms?"

He pulled open the drawer and took out a chain of them, dropping them next to the monitor. "Any more questions?" He didn't wait for her answer, but instantly commanded, "Take off the jeans."

He hooked his fingers into her waistband. She moaned just at the feel of his fingers pressing her belly as he undid the button right below her navel.

"Need some help?" She toed off her Uggs, ripped her fly wide and wiggled the jeans down over her hips.

"God. Karin." He looked at her like she was the most beautiful woman in the world, a look that sent pleasure zipping all through her, a look that banished any leftover nerves about how unsexy her poufy belly and plain white nursing bra must be. He whipped off his thermal shirt. "Finally."

He had one of those universal gyms down in a corner of the garage and he ran on the beach just about every day. Keeping fit really paid off. He was so beautiful, everything sculpted and hard, with that wonderful trail of golden hair leading down to the happy place. And she was so glad—to be here with him, the two of them. Alone in his bedroom.

If they got right on it, they might even manage to have actual sex before Riley woke up.

"Hurry," she begged.

They quickly got rid of the rest of their clothes and

he took her by the shoulders and pulled her down across the bed on top of him.

She laughed as she kissed him, bracing her knees to either side of him, rubbing herself shamelessly against his hard belly, reaching back to wrap her fingers around his thick, hard length.

He groaned when she did that, his hands stroking down her back, grabbing the twin globes of her bottom, holding on tight. He felt so good, so solid and strong. The manly scent of him tempted her, promising all the pleasures she remembered so well. She'd missed this, the two of them, naked, together. Missed it so much.

She wanted him all over her, covering every inch of her. "I want you on top of me."

"Done." He rolled them, taking the top position. She wrapped herself around him like a vine.

He kept on kissing her, a kiss so hot it could burn the house down, a kiss that went on forever, his tongue claiming her mouth, his body covering hers.

This. Right now. With him. It just didn't get any better.

He scattered more kisses, across her cheek, down the side of her throat, stopping to nip at her collarbone, sucking her skin against his teeth. She'd have marks there in the morning.

But so what? She had turtlenecks. And every kiss thrilled her. It all felt just perfect. Exactly right.

"I missed you," she cried. It was a confession, one she couldn't hold back.

He caught her face in his hands again. "I'm here. Here to stay."

"Oh, Liam." Better not to talk about it. Better just to grab this moment and squeeze every drop of joy from it.

His palmed her breasts. She moaned at the pleasurable ache. "Fuller," he said, his voice rich with approval.

She winced. "I'm leaking."

He pulled back enough to grin down at her. "Shut up. You're beautiful." And he took her mouth yet again, spearing his tongue in, sweeping along the edges of her teeth, drinking her down.

When he broke that kiss, it was only to press his lips to her chin, her neck, the hollow of her throat. He dropped a chain of kisses between her breasts. Moving lower, he kissed her belly and the soft points of her hip bones.

And then, easing her thighs over his shoulders and settling between them, he kissed her in the most intimate way. He made her crazy with his lips and little nips of his teeth, with his talented tongue, while his clever fingers played her so perfectly.

It felt so good. She tossed her head against the pillow, whispering his name, moaning it out loud more than once, threading her fingers in his hair, pulling him closer, urging him on.

He eased her legs wider, kissed her more deeply, continuing to stroke her with those skilled strong fingers of his, driving her toward the peak until she gave it up to him, gave herself over completely.

She cried his name as she came.

Had she passed out from sheer ecstasy?

It was just possible.

He moved away. She forced her heavy eyes open and saw he was up on his knees between her wide-open thighs, rolling on one of the condoms.

She reached for him. "Liam. Come here."

He didn't have to be told twice. With care, he lowered

himself to her, gathering her into him, taking her mouth again. She tasted her own musky arousal on his lips.

And she was lost again in the glory of it, kissing him hungrily, reaching down between them, taking him— carefully, so as not to rip the condom—in her hand, guiding him to her.

He surged in hard. She rose up to meet him with a deep, needful groan, lifting her legs and wrapping them good and tight around his lean waist.

After that, he took over, hard and fast at first, so that she could only hold on and let it happen, let him sweep her away into a world of pure, perfect sensation. But then he slowed. He rocked her in a steady, thrilling glide, going deep and then pulling back—only to return to her, over and over again, stoking the heat within her, fanning the fire.

She hit the crest so suddenly, chanting his name, pulling him closer, tighter, as another finish rocked her.

There was a lull. She closed her eyes with a sigh.

But then he started moving again and it felt so good, so right. Her body responded instantly. Another fulfill-ment spun into being from the embers of the last.

Liam stayed with her, whispering encouragements, urging her to take what she needed from him. Sweet bolts of pleasure unfurled within her, spreading out from her core, flowing down her arms, along her legs, bringing hot shivers to the backs of her knees and the soles of her feet. Until every part of her had been swept up, spun around, carried away into complete satisfac-tion.

And then it was his turn. He thrust in hard and so deep—and stilled. She felt his finish claiming him. Wrapping her arms around him, she cradled him close as his climax rolled through him.

There was stillness. She shut her eyes and sank into the lovely, floating feeling of ease. Of peace.

A few minutes later, he got up to take care of the condom. Returning with a cool, wet cloth, he gently bathed her breasts and down her belly. It felt wonderful, that cloth, cooling and soothing, too.

Her eyes were so heavy. She hadn't realized how tired she was. He left her again. She shook herself awake and started to get up.

But then he was there. He came down to the bed with her and pulled the covers over them, gathering her into him.

"I should get Riley, go home." She kissed the side of his throat.

"Not yet." His lips brushed her ear.

She rested her head on his shoulder, listened to his heart beat deep and steady. So soothing, that sound. "If I don't go, I may never move from this spot."

He stroked her hair, smoothing it away from her cheek. "Stay. Just for a minute or two…"

When she opened her eyes, her baby was crying. She tried to push back the covers.

But the hard, warm arms wrapped around her held her even tighter. He nuzzled a kiss in her hair. "I'll get him, bring him to you."

"I have to go, Liam. What time is it, anyway?"

"A little after one…"

She pushed at his chest. "Gotta go."

He kissed the tip of her nose. "He's going to be hungry. You can feed him. And then you can go."

She looked up to meet his eyes. His white teeth flashed with his grin. "Well, go on, then," she said. "Go get him."

He kissed her nose a second time, slid out from under the covers and turned on the lamp. She squinted against the sudden light and brought up a hand to shield her eyes.

"We'll be right back." Stark naked, he headed for the door.

She shoved the covers away and lowered her bare feet to the rug. Shivering a little, she darted around, snatching up her clothes from the floor, from the chair and from the foot of the bed.

Riley kept crying—in stereo—on the monitor and from the room next-door. "Whoa, buddy." She heard Liam groan. "That's quite a load." She paused after pulling on her sweater to watch the monitor as he carried the yowling infant away from the crib and out of sight.

But she could hear him clearly as he continued to murmur reassurances and promises that everything was going to be fine. Riley wasn't going for it. Every time she thought he might settle down a little, he'd suck in a big breath and start bawling again.

Once she'd thrown on her clothes, she crossed the hall and stood in the doorway of the baby's room. "Thanks for taking on the hazardous waste."

He turned to her with the still-crying Riley cradled against his broad, bare chest. "Hey. It's in the job description."

She held out her arms. "My turn." He passed her the squirming baby and she carried him to the easy chair in the corner. Once she was settled, she put Riley to her breast.

A hearty eater, he latched right on.

She glanced up at the naked man standing over her. "Hear that?"

"Silence," he replied with a nod. "It really is golden."

Showing no inclination to go put some clothes on, he studied her face, his gaze moving from her eyes to her lips and back to her eyes again. "I want to lock you in this house and never let you go."

Did she feel a little thrill at that hungry look he wore, at the low roughness of his voice? Absolutely.

But she gave him an easy shrug. "I think they call that kidnapping. It's frowned upon by law enforcement. And people who get kidnapped don't like it much, either."

"Buzzkill," he whispered tenderly. "Next you'll be saying I should go get dressed."

"Never." She gave him a slow once-over. "You look so good naked."

He braced a hand on the back of the chair and bent close for a quick, hard kiss. "I'll leave you alone." He laid his palm gently on Riley's head, cradling it, encompassing it—but just for a moment. And then he turned for the door.

She smiled as she watched him walk away. Not only did he look amazing, he was funny and good to her. And every time he kissed her, she wanted to hold on tight and never, ever let go.

But that would be rushing things, that would be getting all caught up in big emotions, making life-changing decisions without using her head.

Forever was a long, long time. If she ever headed down that road again, she would be 100 percent certain she'd taken the right turn.

Chapter Ten

Otto came to the cottage that morning, as usual, before dawn. Liam turned on the tree lights and the fire. They sat on the hearth with their full mugs of coffee.

"Karin didn't come in until almost two this morning," Otto remarked in a tone so offhand as to be almost humorous.

"What? You stayed awake waiting for her to come home?"

"The habits of a lifetime, my boy. They never die."

Liam sipped his coffee. "I got orders not to talk to you about what is or isn't going on between Karin and me."

"What she doesn't know won't hurt her."

Liam scoffed. "Easy for you to say. You're her dad. She trusts you absolutely. I'm the interloper."

"Just ask her to marry you. It can't be that complicated."

"Otto. You have no idea."

"I'm on your side. So's Coco. And Sten. Madison, too. I think you've even turned Ben around."

He perked up at that. "Ben? Really?"

"Really."

That felt damn good, to think he and Ben were on the right track now. "And Madison, too, huh? Well, she is my sister. She *should* be on my side—even if we hardly know each other." Liam had only talked to the newfound Bravo briefly, at a couple of family dinners back in the spring when she first came to town to meet the family. "It's not right, that I hardly know my own sister."

Otto raised his mug in a quick salute. "You'll get your chance, soon as she and Sten move home to stay."

"You really think she's giving up her career? I read somewhere that she makes millions a year."

"They say money isn't everything."

"They say a lot of things."

"That's right. Because they're true—and yeah. I think Madison is going to finish out those final projects she couldn't get out of and settle right here on Sweetheart Cove, have a few babies, make a good life with Sten. Just like you and Karin need to do."

Liam stared straight ahead. "Not talking to you about Karin."

"Come over for breakfast, why don't you?"

"For a guy who's supposed to leave it alone, you're damn persistent—and no. Even I'm not *that* pushy."

"Karin said to ask you."

"Stop yanking my chain."

"I'm not. She was up with RG when I headed over here. She said, 'Tell Liam we're having waffles and he's welcome to join us…'"

Liam got up, grabbed his phone from where he'd left it on the coffee table and texted Karin. Your dad says I'm invited for breakfast. He glanced back at Otto. "You want more coffee?"

"Yeah."

Karin answered as he was passing the tree to get the pot from the kitchen. What? You didn't believe him?

Should I?

Liam, please join us for breakfast. Today. Tomorrow. Any morning the mood strikes.

Damn. This was progress. It was going to work out for them. She would get past her fear that he would do her the way Bud had. She was learning to trust again.

He just had to curb his impatience, take it one step at a time.

I'll be there.

She sent back a thumbs-up. He stared at that simple emoji and felt like he'd just won the lottery. Or maybe free soloed up El Capitan and lived to tell about it.

"Told you," said Otto with a self-satisfied smirk. "Now bring that pot over here. I need my caffeine."

At breakfast, he behaved himself. Mostly. Now and then, he would catch himself staring too long at Karin, but he didn't think he was all that obvious.

That night, she came over with Riley as soon as the kids were in bed. She'd nursed him at the other house and when she put him in his crib at the cottage, he didn't even make a peep.

They had a couple of hours, the two of them, in bed. It was so good with her. He got now why some guys never looked at another woman.

Why would he want to look at someone else when he could spend every free moment staring at Karin, talking to Karin, laughing with her, kissing her, having great sex with her?

Sunday morning, he went to breakfast at the main house again. Karin gave him that certain smile, the one that was only for him. After they ate, he helped Coco with cleanup.

She was Batgirl today, rattling off her special powers, leaning in close to ask with completely adorable and uncharacteristic shyness, "Are you still taking me to see the trucks today, Liam?"

"You still want to go?"

"Yes, please!"

"Can you be ready at nine?"

"Yes, I can!"

Karin took him aside to remind him that Coco was only seven and tended to trust everyone she met. She needed closer supervision than nine-year-old, super mature, overly cautious Ben.

"I hear you," he promised. "I won't let her out of my sight."

Coco wore her black tights and yellow rain boots for the trip, but Karin insisted that she switch out her towel cape for a coat and a warm wool hat. The red hat had a border of snowflakes and a big, white pom-pom that bounced all the way to Bravo Trucking. Coco pretty much talked nonstop.

She charmed everyone in the driver's lounge. Liam hung out with her there for half an hour or so, took her for a quick tour of the offices and the fuel island and then out to have a look at the engine of one of the trucks.

He showed her how to pop the hood latches and then how easily the giant hood opened with a tug on the front. When he launched into his spiel about how the engine worked, she stared up at him as though transfixed by his every word.

"Questions?" he asked once he'd given her a quick rundown.

"Um, no." Those blue eyes were so serious. "But I would really like to go for a ride in this truck, Liam."

"Now?"

Her pom-pom bobbed and her smile bloomed wide. "Yes, now, please!" She looked up at him like he'd grabbed her a handful of stars. "I'm glad you're our baby's daddy, Liam."

All of a sudden, he felt kind of choked up. "Me, too."

"I think you should get married to Mommy and we can all live happily ever after like in *The Wild Swans* and *Frozen* and *Beauty and the Beast*."

Me, too! But that time he didn't say it out loud. A guy had to be careful about the promises he made. Especially to children.

Coco had her head tipped to the side now. She stared up at him, frowning a little. "Maybe you should just think about it?"

"I will—now, how 'bout that ride?"

Liam boosted her up into the cab and took the wheel.

They circled the terminal and she pointed out the buildings she'd visited. When they got back where they'd started, she wasn't ready to quit, so he drove her across the Youngs Bay Bridge and into Astoria. They rumbled along Marine Drive, circling back using Commercial.

On the way home to Valentine Bay, they stopped at the same diner he and Ben had eaten at the week before. Coco wanted the works, a burger, chocolate milkshake and fries. She only managed to eat about half of all that before she wiped her mouth with her napkin and gave him one of those looks she was an absolute master at—one of those I'm-the-cutest-little-girl-in-the-universe looks.

"It was really good, Liam, but I'm *really* full. My eyes are bigger than my tummy. That's what Grandpa always says. But Mommy says we have to practice not wasting food."

"We'll take it to go."

"The milkshake will melt."

Was he getting played? It was starting to seem like a definite possibility. "Hmm. Looks like you already ate most of the milkshake."

"It's my favorite." She grinned so wide, he could see the gap on the bottom where she'd lost two baby teeth. The white rims of her grown-up teeth had just begun to show. "I like chocolate milkshakes more than french fries and a *lot* more than a hamburger."

Liam leaned in and lowered his voice to secret-sharing level. "What are you telling me that you're not telling me?"

She giggled. "You're funny, Liam."

"Did you do something you shouldn't have done?"

"Not exac'ly."

"So then, what's going on?"

Her little shoulders sagged. "Well, Mommy usually says if they don't have a mini-burger and a small-size fries, I should just skip the fries. And the milkshake was kind of big, too. I was afraid to ask for a mini-shake because maybe they don't have those and even if they do, I would rather have a big one."

Wouldn't we all? "So you broke the rules about wasting food, is that what you're telling me?"

Those eyes were enormous in that little pixie face with that perfect pointed chin just like her mom's. "Umm-hmm."

How big of a deal was this, really? He had no idea. It was all way above his pay grade, parenting-wise. "I'm not about to make you take the leftovers home."

She brightened. "You're not?"

"I'll just tell your mom that I didn't know the rules and I let you order too much food."

"Liam," she chided. "That's not gonna work with my mom."

"Why not?"

"'Cause my mom knows that *I* know the rules and I'm s'posed to follow them—and you know what? I'll just take the leftovers home."

He kept his expression carefully neutral though a grin was trying really hard to stretch the edges of his mouth. "You sure?"

"Umm-hmm. It's okay if I order too much food as long as I eat the leftovers later."

"Problem solved, then?"

"Yeah, 'cept I have to eat the leftovers."

"Life is full of choices."

She wrinkled her little nose at him. "That's exac'ly what Mommy says."

That night, Karin came over again. She'd left RG sleeping at the other house. Her dad would call when he needed her. "Sorry. I probably won't be staying all that long."

"I'll take you however I can get you." He caught her hand, pulled her into his arms and walked her backward down the hall to the bedroom, kissing her all the way. They made love fast and hard, with no preamble, rolling around on the bed, holding on to each other good and tight. It was great.

And then, when Otto didn't call, they started again, this time making it last, indulging in deep, lazy kisses and slow, sweet caresses. After that second time, they talked.

"Coco can wrap the average adult around her pinkie finger," Karin said. She was lying on her back, the covers pulled up over those breasts he loved to kiss, curling a lock of her hair around one of her fingers. "But you nailed the leftovers issue. Well done."

Feeling contented, happy with the world and everything in it, he scooted a little closer to her side of the bed, braced up on an elbow and just let himself enjoy looking at her, breathing in the sweet scent of her that was a little bit musky from all the fun they'd been having. "I wouldn't say I nailed anything. I just let her talk herself into doing the right thing."

"You're good with kids." She gave him a teasing little smile. "You're going to make some lucky woman the perfect husband."

And just like that, in the space of a few seconds, all his easy contentment vanished. "What the hell is that supposed to mean, Karin?"

"Whoa." She rolled to her side and faced him fully. "What'd I say?"

"You want to see me with another woman?"

"Liam, come on. Of course not." She brushed his shoulder with a tentative hand. He had to consciously hold himself still in order not to jerk away from her. "It was just a figure of speech."

Impatience rose inside him, making his skin feel too tight and his pulse throb like an infected wound. "Sometimes I think you don't take me seriously."

"That's not true." She ran her palm down the outside of his arm, petting him. Soothing him.

It worked. To a degree.

But she'd reopened this can of worms and damned if he was just going to shove the lid back on and pretend nothing had happened. "I don't want *some* woman, Karin. I want *you.*"

She put a finger to his lips. "Liam, come on, don't…"

Gently, he guided her hand away from his mouth. "Marry me."

She just looked at him. Her eyes were a thousand years old.

He said it again. "Marry me."

"Because of Riley," she whispered bleakly.

"Yeah. Because of our son. What's wrong with that? Because of Riley and because I want you and I don't want to be with anyone but you. And because of Coco and Ben. Hell, because of Otto. We can make a good life. We can make it all work."

"Don't." She touched his mouth again. "Please."

"Because I lov—"

"No." She glared at him. "Uh-uh. Don't say it. I really and truly do not want to hear it."

He sat up and swung his legs over the edge of the bed—at which point he realized he was staying right here. Because there was nowhere he wanted to be but with her. Even when he was mad at her, he didn't want to walk away from her.

And she had it right. He shouldn't have started in

with this, shouldn't have let himself lose it over some offhand remark of hers.

Behind him, the bed shifted as she rose to her knees.

She touched him. He felt her tentative hand on his shoulder. "Liam." He felt...everything. Her touch, her body behind him, so smooth and soft; her breath caressing the back of his neck. "Liam, I'm sorry. That was a crappy thing I said. I want you, too. I do. I would be so jealous if you went out and found someone else. You're important to me. So much so that it scares me."

"There's nothing for you to be scared of. I'm not Bud. I've had my time to be free, to keep things casual and easy, to answer to no one but myself. I know what I want now and I want to be with you. I want to answer to you, Karin, and to be responsible for you. I want to be the one they have to call if you're in need."

"And I want to be with *you*. So much. But I'm not just jumping into something permanent. I'm never doing that again. I'm not ready to go making promises about forever. I just need to take it one day at a time. And I do love this—you and me, together. Like this. I love how you are with me. And with Riley. With my family. It's only that sometimes it kind of feels like it's too good to be true, you know?"

He shook his head and a humorless chuckle escaped him. "Do you hear yourself? You like everything about me. You just don't believe I'm for real."

"Look, I've got issues, I know it. I'm not blind to myself, to who I am. I'm not the easiest woman to be with. I'm not trusting. I've got...defenses. And I guess I'm always half expecting you to figure out that I'm a pain in the ass and this thing with us just doesn't work for you."

Her hand was still on his shoulder. He reached up and laid his over it, sliding his thumb in under her fingers to rub the soft heart of her palm. "I'm going nowhere. How am I going to convince you of that?"

"Liam…" It was barely a whisper. She moved in closer behind him, pulling her hand out from under his, but not to retreat. To get closer. She pressed her soft breasts against him, wrapped her arms around his belly and rested her cheek on his shoulder. "Liam."

All he had to do was turn his head. Her sweet mouth was right there. She smelled of citrus and rain and baby lotion. She smelled like all the best things, everything he'd ever wanted all wrapped up in one contrary, difficult, big-eyed, wild-haired woman.

I love you, Karin.

No, he didn't say it. She didn't want to hear it. But he thought it, thought it over and over, as he kissed her.

I love you.

He turned and curved his body over her, carrying her down to the bed again, sweeping his hands along her arms, into the silky curve of her waist, down over her smooth thighs, parting her, touching her, so slick and wet, already primed for him.

I love you.

She reached down between them and curled her hand around him, taking command of him. He groaned his pleasure into their kiss as she stroked him, tightly, forcefully. A little bit roughly.

Just the way he liked it.

He reached out, grabbed a condom from the nightstand, managed to get the thing unwrapped. She helped him, taking it from him, rolling it down over his aching length.

I love you.

The words were there, in his head, pulsing with the beat of his heart as he sank into her. As she wrapped herself around him, pulling him tightly to her, so good. So right.

I love you.

As he moved within her, rocking her slowly, taking her higher and higher.

I love you.

As she came apart, chanting his name.

Chapter Eleven

After the night she wouldn't let him say the *L* word, Liam tried to keep his focus on the good things.

Like how Karin couldn't stay away from him. She appeared at his door five or six nights out of seven and she stayed for an hour or two, at least—sometimes much longer.

But she always returned home before the kids woke up. And she continued to insist that they keep their relationship just between the two of them. He hated her restrictions, like she was keeping him in his place, not letting him get too close.

Most Sundays, he went to dinner at Daniel's. It was a Bravo family tradition. He'd tried several times to get her to come with him, to bring the kids and Otto, too. She always had some reason why it just wouldn't work. He asked her again the second Friday in December. Riley was asleep in the crib at the cottage and they were sitting by the fire in the main room.

She sipped the last of her raspberry tea and answered regretfully, "Thanks, but I don't think so, Liam."

"Just one time," he coaxed. "This Sunday."

"Your brother and his wife do not need a bunch of extra people descending on them."

"Yeah, Karin. They do. Especially if it's you and the kids and Otto. You were there at Thanksgiving. They loved having you. You're welcome there anytime."

She set her empty mug down, leaned in and kissed him. "Thanks, but no."

"Then how about Christmas? Come to Daniel's for dinner Christmas Day."

"Liam…"

He pulled her close and kissed the tip of her nose. "Don't answer now. Think about."

"I just don't…"

He covered her lips with his before she could dish out another denial. She seemed only too happy for the distraction. He gathered her closer and deepened the kiss. Then, pulling her up with him, he led her down the hall to his bedroom. As he dragged her down on the bed with him, he reminded himself that he was focusing on the positive, looking for the good things in what he had with her.

Kissing her. Holding her. Having her in his bed…

These were very good things.

And the sex was by no means all of the goodness.

He loved the way she trusted him with Coco and Ben—and seemed to count on him, too. She didn't hesitate to ask him to ferry them around or keep an eye on them when Otto was at the Boatworks and she needed to run over to the store. Who knew he'd ever be the kind of guy who couldn't wait to drive the kids to play dates and sleepovers, to take Coco to her Hip-Hoppin' Dance Class and Ben to Science Club?

The next week, he even managed to get himself an invite to the Valentine Bay Elementary School Christmas show wherein Coco played a singing, dancing snowflake and Ben wore a beard, a yellow robe and a crown as one of the Three Wise Men. Liam was so proud of them, he was first on his feet to lead the standing ovation when they all came out and took their bows.

Every morning, he showed up at the main house with Otto for breakfast. And every morning, Karin smiled at him like she was glad to see him. He kept waiting for the day when she'd move in close, maybe offer her sweet mouth for a quick kiss, the day when she'd say something soft and low and welcoming, just between the two of them.

But the mornings went by, one by one, and a more intimate breakfast greeting didn't happen. He told himself that it *would* happen. Someday very soon. He just needed to stay positive. She would get over her fear of giving her heart to him.

They would be together. *Really* together. Live in the same house, sleep in the same bed—and not just for a few stolen hours, either. Uh-uh. Same bed.

All. Night. Long.

Negativity crept in, though. Sometimes he couldn't help thinking that all he'd ever had of Karin Killigan were stolen moments. From last Christmas to now, she fit him in when she could manage it—and yeah, she fit him in just about every night as of now. That was progress, definitely.

But she wouldn't simply let it be known that she was with him.

Even if she wouldn't marry him, she could let him be *more*. More than her baby daddy. More than her co-parent. More than the helpful guy next door. More than the man who made her cry out his name two or three times a night.

Be patient, he kept telling himself.

And he tried, he really did. But his patience was fraying. No matter how often he reminded himself that he and Karin really hadn't been together all that long and that he needed to chill, back off, let her find her way to him in her own time, he couldn't help feeling frustrated.

He'd finally figured out what he wanted out of life and he didn't want to waste a moment going forward. But he was stuck at the threshold of his own happiness, waiting for Karin to open the damn door and let him in.

The kids had the usual two-week holiday break from school. It started the Friday before Christmas.

Karin needed to wrangle them childcare for when she had to be at the Boatworks. They didn't want to spend their Christmas vacation at a winter break camp and they didn't want to hang around the office at the Boatworks with her, either. Usually, her dad and Sten helped her out. But Sten was in LA. And Otto had a couple of big refitting jobs. He couldn't look after them as much as he usually did.

Liam said he would stay home and watch them a couple of days a week, but she turned him down. He already took Riley every Wednesday and Friday till noon. And he had a business—a busy, successful, de-manding one. He needed to spend his workdays running it. He couldn't be hanging around her house looking after the kids.

She had a couple of trusted sitters she'd always used, but both of them were well into their teens now. One had a job flipping burgers and the other was spending her Christmas break at her dad's house in Telluride.

She was kind of at her wit's end with the situation and gearing up to tell Ben and Coco that they were going to have to go to day camp.

And then, Sten and Madison came home.

Sten called on Saturday morning during breakfast to say that Madison had two weeks off from filming the science fiction epic she'd been working on since May. They'd chartered a private jet and would be arriving at Valentine Bay Executive Airport at noon.

At a quarter of one, they showed up at the house in a Lincoln Navigator with Madison's bodyguards, Sergei and Dirk. Everyone was home, including Liam, who'd driven up to Bravo Trucking for a couple of hours that morning, but returned in time to be there to greet the newlyweds.

When Madison emerged from the back seat, her streaky blond hair piled up in a sloppy bun, wearing old jeans and a giant sweater that hung off one shoulder, Coco shouted, "Madison! Merry Christmas!" and ran straight for her. Madison opened her arms and the two of them hugged it out like the best buddies they'd become back in March when the movie star first came to Sweetheart Cove.

Ben went right to Sten for a slightly more restrained greeting. And then there were hugs all around.

Karin grabbed her brother and whispered mock desperately, "Thank God you're here. I need a kidsitter."

He laughed. "Little sister, whatever you need for the next two weeks, you're gonna get it."

* * *

They got the car unloaded and Sten, Madison and the bodyguards settled upstairs in Sten's half of the house. That day, they all mostly just hung out in the downstairs great room around the tree, catching up, taking turns holding Riley and playing board games. Karin kept the Christmas tunes playing in the background. She also cooked a big dinner and they all sat down to eat together.

Once the kids were in bed, Otto headed down to Sten's workshop under the house. He had a few Christmas projects he was working on. Liam invited Madison and Sten over to the cottage for a drink.

"You, too, Karin." He turned those baby blues on her and gave her one of those smiles that melted her midsection. "Bring RG. You can put him to bed over there."

She almost said no, because she didn't want her brother or Madison figuring out how close she and Liam had become—which was a ridiculous excuse, and she knew it. There really was some sense in not letting her kids start to see her and Liam as a couple until they were certain their relationship would last. But Madison and Sten would be fine no matter what happened in the end between Karin and her baby's father.

Karin put on her coat and bundled up the baby and they all five went next door. One of the bodyguards trailed after them to the cottage but didn't follow them inside.

It was nice, really. Riley went right to sleep in his crib. Liam got everyone something to drink and they sat around the fire. It had started snowing, a light snow, one that wouldn't stick on the ground, but they could see it drifting down beyond the windows, lit by the Christmas lights strung in the eaves and along the deck railing, the white flakes spinning in the cold wind.

Madison was all about getting to know Liam better. "It's another of the many crappy things about being switched at birth," she said. "I feel like I have twenty-seven years to make up for. Liam, we should have grown up together. I should know all your quirks and irritating habits and be constantly ragging on you about them." She snuggled up against Sten, who sat beside her on the sofa. "We should be like Sten and Karin."

"Yeah." Sten gave a wry chuckle. "Karin always knows what's best for me. It's really annoying."

No way Karin could let that remark pass. "I'm very wise, actually. I give excellent advice."

"Oh, really?" Liam had taken the seat beside her in front of the fire. She found herself wishing he would put his arm around her—at the same time as she told herself she appreciated his restraint.

Yeah. No doubt about it. She was kind of a mess over him, longing for it to be the real thing with him and simultaneously terrified that it would all blow up in her face—and what were they talking about?

Right. Her willingness to give her big brother advice. "You'd better believe I've given Sten advice. I've made it my mission to set him straight whenever he needs it."

Sten groaned. "Yeah. Whether I want to be set straight or not."

Karin admitted, "Now and then it's just possible that I've been a tiny bit in your face."

"A *tiny bit*?"

"Come on, Sten. Don't give me attitude. You know I was right about you two." Karin raised her ginger beer in a salute to Madison.

Madison asked eagerly, "What did you say to him?"

"Sorry. I can't give you specifics. It was a private conversation between a thickheaded brother and his brilliant, emotionally sensitive and extremely perceptive sister. Let's just say he was scared to take a chance on what he had with you and I helped him to see that he was all wrong."

Now Madison was grinning at Sten. "You *were* scared." She kissed his cheek.

"But I got over it."

"Oh, yes you did." Her voice was soft and she leaned into him. "And magnificently, too."

"Magnificent. That's me, all right." Sten kissed her.

Karin glanced away from the private moment between her brother and his wife—and into Liam's waiting eyes. At least he didn't get on her for her own reluctance to take a chance on love.

Not right then, anyway.

Later, after Sten and Madison had gone back to the other house, Liam locked the door, turned off the lights and led her down the hall to his room.

"I was afraid you'd run right out the door after them," he teased as he took her red sweater by the hem and pulled it off over her head.

She kissed his beard-scruffy, sculpted jaw. "The baby's still sleeping and I want to be here with you—and my brother and Madison are grown-ups. They can think what they want about me and you." She got to work unbuttoning his flannel shirt.

He interrupted her busy fingers long enough to get rid of her bra. Then he tipped up her chin and kissed her, the sweetest kind of kiss, slow and teasing, as she continued to work her way from one button to the next down the front of his shirt.

She slipped the shirt off his fine, broad shoulders. It dropped to the rug.

He asked, "So you challenged your brother to take a chance on love, huh?"

She was just about to kiss him, but defensiveness curled through her as she met his eyes. "Really, it was a completely different situation with Madison and Sten."

Liam dipped his head and whispered in her ear. "Different than what?"

"You know very well what."

He pulled back enough to look at her again. "You mean, different than you and me."

"That's right."

He traced the line of her jaw with a slow pass of his index finger, making her shiver a little, causing that lovely, hollowed-out feeling low in her belly. And he asked, "Specifically, how are Madison and Sten different from you and me?"

"They were both single, no kids involved. It was simpler for them. Less baggage, you know?"

"Kids or not, everybody's got baggage, Karin."

"You're not hearing me."

"Yes, I am." His fingers eased under the fall of her hair and he cupped the back of her neck, rubbing it a little, easing tension she hadn't even realized was there. "When I took Coco to Bravo Trucking, she said you and I should get married and we'd all live happily ever after like in a Disney movie. And as you already know, Ben only wanted me to promise I wasn't going to go away. RG is just a baby, but I have a really strong feeling he's not going to mind if his parents end up married to each other. So I would say the baggage we're talking about isn't really to do with the kids, is it?"

"Of course it's to do with the kids. They're the top

priority—and about Coco saying we ought to get married. How did you answer her?"

He pulled her closer and pressed his lips to the center of her forehead. "Before I could figure out a good answer, she changed her mind and suggested that I just think about it. I said I would. We left it at that."

"Why didn't you tell me this sooner?"

He tipped up her chin so she had to look at him. "Please don't freeze up on me."

"I'm not, I just..." She had no idea what to say next and ended up murmuring weakly, "They're my kids. I don't want them hurt."

"I would never hurt them." He said it sincerely.

And she believed him. "I know." *Not on purpose, anyway.* "And you're right. I do have baggage. Way too much of it."

"You could...let me help you carry it." He gazed down at her so steadily.

She wanted to grab on to him—grab on tight and never let him go.

Because he was so good to her and to her children. Because who did she think she was kidding?

Her heart was already his. And she didn't want to think about that, about how it would all work out in the end, about where they were going and if they would ever actually get there. She just wanted to hold him close and feel his heartbeat next to hers and pretend there was no tomorrow.

Hold him close and lose herself in the glory of right now.

She undid another button. "Liam?"

"Hmm?"

"Kiss me. Now."

His lips touched hers and she slid her hands up to

link behind his neck. All her worries flew away. It was just Liam and Karin, holding on tight, keeping each other warm on a cold winter's night.

"Come with us for Sunday dinner at Daniel's," Madison said the next morning at breakfast. "Let's have the whole family together."

"Yeah." Sten put in his two cents. "Please come."

Coco literally bounced in her chair. "I know I'm not s'posed to interrupt when the grown-ups are deciding things, but just in case you want to know what I think, I think yes! We should go!"

Ben was nodding. "I think so, too," he solemnly intoned.

"I *like* the Bravos," Coco proclaimed. "And I bet they have a big Christmas tree."

Karin slid a glance at Liam. He was looking down, but she knew he was barely hiding a grin. "So Liam. What do you think?"

He glanced up at last and she took the full force of his sky blue gaze. "I'll say it again. I want you all to come to Sunday dinner at Daniel's."

How could she keep saying no when he looked at her that way?

She couldn't. And she didn't.

That afternoon, she packed up plenty of cookies and Christmas candy and the leftover ham from the night before and off they went to the Bravo house on Rhinehart Hill. They took two cars, Liam's F-150 and the Navigator, with one of the bodyguards behind the wheel.

Once they got there, Karin wondered why she'd ever said no. Everyone really did seem happy to see them. She'd always enjoyed hanging out with Liam's sisters, and the giant Christmas tree in the family room was a beautiful sight to behold.

She got to touch base with Connor and Aly Bravo, who'd just returned from New York, where Aly had finished up at her longtime job there, sublet her apartment— and married Connor for the second time.

Aly asked to hold Riley. She sighed when Karin laid him in her arms. "He is just perfect." Connor's bride glanced up with a glowing smile. "Connor and I are expecting in May."

"Wow. Congratulations."

"What can I say? It was unexpected, but we aren't complaining. We both always wanted kids."

Aly had five brothers, one of whom had been born just a couple of months ago. Of her older brothers, two were married with children and Dante, the oldest, was divorced with twin daughters. Aly said that she and Connor would be spending Christmas Day at her parents' house and Christmas Eve right here on Rinehart Hill with the Bravos.

"It's good to be home." Aly smiled dreamily down at Riley. "I love New York. But for me, there's nothing like Christmas in Valentine Bay."

A little later, Keely, Daniel's wife, pulled Karin aside and invited her and the kids and her dad for Christmas dinner. "I'm sure Liam's already asked you, but I just wanted you to know how much we'd all love it if you guys would join us for Christmas Day, too."

Karin shocked the hell out of herself and almost said yes on the spot. After all, Sten and Madison would be coming here to the Bravo house, as would Liam. She and her dad and the kids might as well come, too. But her reluctance to get swept up in too much togetherness with Liam and his family won out. She thanked Keely and promised to talk to Liam about it.

It was after nine when Karin glanced over and saw that Coco had fallen asleep on the floor in front of the tree.

She leaned close to Liam and whispered, "Time to go."

Leaving Sten and Madison and the bodyguards behind, Karin, Liam, Otto and the kids headed for home.

Once they got everyone into the house, Otto said, "Give me that baby."

Karin didn't argue. She passed him the baby carrier in which Riley slept, his chin on his chest, drooling a little.

Her dad said, "I'll put the kids to bed. There's milk in the fridge if RG here gets hungry. You two have a nice night."

"So much for not letting anybody know we're together," she grumbled to Liam several minutes later. They were already in his bedroom, under the covers, cuddled up close.

"You're the one who's all tied in knots over that," he reminded her.

She used her fingers to comb his hair back off his forehead. "I'm...getting used to it."

He ducked close, pressed his mouth to her neck—and blew a raspberry against the side of her throat. When she laughed and wriggled away, he said, "Good. Because I really am going nowhere—as I've said so many times I've lost count."

She cuddled in close again. "Keely invited us all to Christmas dinner."

He slid an arm under her shoulders and drew her closer still. "And you said...?"

"That I would talk to you about it."

"And…?"

Really, why hold out against having Christmas at Daniel and Keely's house? Her family loved going over there. And so did she. "Sure. Let's spend the afternoon at Daniel's."

He tipped up her chin and stared into her eyes. "Tell me I'm not dreaming. Tell me you just said yes to Christmas dinner with the Bravos."

"Yes, I said yes."

He kissed the tip of her nose. "That wasn't so hard, now was it?"

She laughed. "You are impossible."

"But in the best kind of way, right?"

"Oh, absolutely." She settled her head on his shoulder. "I do like this, Liam. You and me, how it's all kind of working out."

"We're making progress, together." He breathed the words into her hair.

"Umm-hmm." Held safe in his arms, she shut her eyes and let herself relax completely. It really was getting easier, day by day, to put the past behind her, to start letting herself imagine a future with Liam.

Yes, at first it had seemed far too similar to the situation she'd gotten herself into with Bud—a baby on the way and a man just trying to step up and do right. But Liam really did seem to like being a family man. And he really did seem to care for her. Not to mention, she was so completely in love with him.

In love with Liam.

Just thinking those words sent a warning shiver through her, no matter that she'd grown increasingly sure they were true.

It wasn't something she felt entirely ready to deal

with yet. And she certainly wouldn't be saying I love you out loud to him.

Not yet. Not until…

Who knew? She didn't. But it was going to take some time yet, before she would be willing to declare her love to Liam. Right now, she couldn't even let *him* say the words.

Right now, what she felt for him was for her to know and no one else to find out. She needed more time to become absolutely certain that what they had together really was as strong and enduring as she had started to let herself hope it might be.

Liam drove down to his Portland offices early the next day for a couple of meetings. He was finished before noon and decided to make a detour into downtown, do a little Christmas shopping at an upscale mall called Pioneer Place.

He picked up a few things for Coco and Ben on the first level and then rode the escalator up to the second. If he remembered correctly, there was a certain jewelry story up there.

Tiffany & Co.

He spotted it right away and a feeling of satisfaction spread through him as he thought of Karin. They were getting it together, him and Karin. They had a happy, healthy baby boy and every day he felt more a part of the Larson-Killigan family.

Her kids and her dad trusted him. And Sten had been on his side from the first, not even hesitating to lease him the cottage all those weeks and weeks ago, when he was a brand-new dad, desperate for a closer connection to his son and to the frustrating, unforgettable woman who was so determined not to let him get near.

Maybe it was a little early to go browsing engagement rings.

But hey, how often did he get anywhere near Tiffany & Co.? Pretty much never.

What could it hurt just to look?

Someday soon, he'd be needing the right ring. And when that happened, it would damn well be the best.

Inside the store, there were fancy wreaths on the walls, a tree all decked out with Tiffany-blue lights and white satin bows. Christmas music played, turned down tastefully low, like a hum of holiday cheer in the background. He was greeted by the guard at the door and by a couple of salespeople. A pretty woman with pale blond hair asked if there was something or someone in particular he was shopping for.

He shook his head. "Just looking."

"Ah. Take your time. Let me know if there's anything I can do to help."

He thanked her and browsed the big, gleaming cases of engagement and wedding rings, each one more sparkly and beautiful than the one before it.

It was a little overwhelming—until he saw *the* ring. It was simple and perfect, with a gorgeous square diamond glittering so brightly on a platinum band.

The blonde stepped near again. In a soft, pleasant voice, she began talking about responsible sourcing, about the four C's of diamonds—carat, cut, color and clarity.

He looked up and grinned at her. "I want that one, and the platinum band with the diamonds for the wedding ring…"

* * *

Liam left Tiffany & Co. feeling equal parts exhilarated and stunned. He'd just bought a matched pair of sparklers that cost more than his truck.

And he'd honestly only gone in there to look.

But hey. When he finally did get down on one knee and offer his ring to Karin along with his heart and all his worldly possessions, she was going to love that ring.

And if the impossible happened and the perfect ring wasn't right for her, the nice saleswoman had assured him that he could bring Karin in to choose something else.

So it was nothing to get freaky over. He'd wanted the best for Karin and he'd gotten the best.

And for now, he had a plan: do nothing. Not for a while. He would put the perfect rings away, enjoy the rest of the holiday season and wait for the right moment, no matter how long it took to get there.

Karin was skittish about love, about marriage. He knew that. He *got* that. He honestly did. He understood her fears and her doubts. The catastrophe of her first marriage still haunted her. And she needed a whole lot of time to learn to trust that he was all in with her the way Bud had never really been.

His phone buzzed with a text just as he reached the parking garage a block from the mall. It was Karin.

Pork chops tonight. 6 o'clock. Interested?

He wore a giant grin as he paused on the sidewalk to answer. I'll be there.

Dinner was great. RG was up, so Liam ate with the baby on his lap. Sten and Madison joined them. Afterward, Coco dragged Liam into her room and whipped out a pink plastic pitcher, her Christmas gift for Karin.

"Isn't it beautiful, Liam? Won't Mommy just love it?"

He agreed that it was one fine-looking pitcher and Karin would be so happy to have it. Next, he checked in with Ben to see how he was doing on his latest project for Science Club.

Around eight, he returned to the cottage and headed straight for the wall safe in the bedroom closet to check out his Tiffany purchase. A part of him still didn't quite believe he'd just gone out and done it—bought Karin a ring.

But he had. And it was freaking gorgeous.

He'd just stuck the tiny black velvet box into the blue Tiffany box and then back into the safe and returned to the main room when she showed up at the slider.

He shoved open the door and she came straight into his arms like there was no place on earth she would rather be. "Dad shooed me out again. He promised to look after RG and make sure Ben and Coco get to bed on time."

"Otto's my hero."

"Mine, too." She sighed and tipped up her mouth in an invitation to a kiss. It was an invitation he accepted with enthusiasm.

Damn, she was beautiful. She just seemed to glow with happiness, so easy and comfortable with him, with the world, with the life they were making, day by day, the two of them—even if she hadn't quite gotten to where she would admit that out loud.

They hung out in the main room for a while, enjoying the fire, discussing Christmas Eve, which they would share at the other house with the kids and Otto, Sten and Madison. Christmas morning, he would cook breakfast for everyone here at the cottage. Then they would return to the main house to open presents.

And then, as she'd miraculously agreed the night before, they would head up to Rhinehart Hill for Christmas dinner with his family.

Life didn't get any better than this.

He scooped her up in his arms and headed down the hall to his bedroom, where he made love to her slowly, his mind and heart overflowing with words of love.

Words that he really didn't intend to try to say out loud again. Not yet.

But she was moving beneath him, sighing his name, those blue-green eyes shining as she gazed up at him through the dark, thick fringe of her eyelashes. All that coffee-brown hair was spread out on the pillow, tangled and wild. He wanted to capture the moment, never let it go.

And then she said it, so soft and low he might not have heard it if he hadn't been staring directly down at her beautiful face. "I love you so much, Liam. I love you. I do."

And it was like a dam breaking inside him, the words spilling out of him, the ones she'd never let him say before. "I love you, Karin. You're everything to me…"

Afterward, she seemed kind of quiet, but she tucked herself in nice and close to him. Idly, she traced the shape of his ear, brushed her fingers along his jaw, combed them up into his hair.

He pressed a kiss to the curve of her shoulder and she made a soft little sound in her throat. It sounded like approval. Affection.

Love.

And he just couldn't do it. Couldn't wait another day,

another hour, another minute to ask her, to promise her everything, to give her the ring he'd chosen for her.

He kissed her shoulder again and breathed in the incomparable scent of her skin. "Do not move from this spot."

She let out a throaty little moan. "No worries. I don't think I *can* move. I just might be in an after-sex coma."

He chuckled. "Try to stay conscious. I'll be right back." He slid out from under the covers and turned for the closet.

"Liam, what—?"

"Just wait. You'll see." He pulled open the closet door, switched on the light and shoved a row of shirts to the side. Four quick pokes at the keypad and he had the safe open. The blue box was waiting. He took out the black velvet box inside and returned with it to the bed.

She was sitting up by then, clutching the sheet to her chest. "What are you up to?"

He dropped to a knee, held out the tiny box and flipped the lid back.

She stared down at the ring, eyes big as sand dollars. "Liam."

"Marry me, Karin."

She just kept staring, clutching the sheet even tighter. "I, um, that's the most gorgeous ring I've ever seen."

"Say yes."

She winced—she actually winced at him. "Liam. I'm so sorry. I can't do that. You know I can't. Not right now."

Chapter Twelve

Karin sincerely hated herself at that moment.

Liam stared up at her from where he knelt on the rug, a frown creasing his brow. He flipped the box shut, fisted his hand around it and let his arm drop to his side. "You said you love me."

"I know. And I do, but…" Really, what was he supposed to think? "I'm sorry," she babbled. "I shouldn't have said it. I didn't mean to say it."

He rose and set the magnificent ring in its velvet box on the nightstand. And then he just stood there by the bed, so tall and strong, wearing nothing but a somber expression, his eyes full of shadows and sadness now. "You didn't mean to say you love me?"

"No! I… Well, of course, I…" She stopped, forced herself to take a slow breath, and tried again. "I do love you, even though I tried really hard not to."

He almost smiled, but then his fine mouth flattened out again. "No kidding."

"I fell for you, Liam. I've fallen. I'm just gone on you. I wasn't going to tell you, though. Not until I was ready to, um, move on to the next step. But it's been so good between us lately. And tonight was so perfect and beautiful and true. I got carried away, I guess. The words just slipped out. I'm so sorry."

One golden-brown eyebrow inched upward. "Sorry that you love me?"

Could she *be* more confusing? "Please. No. That's not what I mean." She reached out and took his hand. He didn't exactly give it to her, but he let her have it, he didn't jerk away. "Come back to bed."

He stared at her so strangely, like she'd hurt him so bad, broken something inside him. "Karin. Are you gonna talk to me about this? Tell me, honestly, why you keep refusing to take a chance on us?"

"Please..." She tugged on his hand. "Come here."

He gave in and got back under the covers with her. They propped their pillows against the headboard and sat up, side by side. "Okay," he said. "Talk."

She put her fingers to her temples and rubbed to ease the tension that caused a dull throbbing behind her eyes. "I just have to be sure that we can really make it work before there are rings and promises of forever. I have to be 100 percent certain. I can't take a chance that I'll mess up again. It's just not fair to the kids—or to you, really. Some things, you can't come back from, Liam."

"You have to know that you're never going to get the certainty you say you need. When you love another person, you're always taking a risk. There are no guarantees."

What could she say to that? She knew he was right.

He held her gaze. "So, Karin. Take a chance. On me. On us."

A frustrated cry escaped her. "But horrible things can happen. You have no idea."

"Yeah, I do. When he was only eight years old, my brother disappeared in Siberia, vanished without a trace never to be seen or heard from again. Two years later, my mom and dad died in a Thailand tsunami. Believe me, I know about horrible things."

Shame made her cheeks burn. "Oh, my God. You're right. Of course, you know exactly what I'm talking about. And I am so sorry—about Finn, about your dad and mom. Could I *be* any more insensitive?" She covered her face with her hands.

"Hey. Look at me."

She dropped her hands and made herself face him. "Yeah?"

"Bad shit happens. To everyone. And for you, that means Bud, right? You're trying to tell me that you're not really over his death, that he's always going to be a barrier between us?"

"Not in the way that you think. It's not like I'm in love with his memory or anything. Liam, what haunts me is that I rushed into marriage with him and it all went to hell. Everybody got hurt—my children included. I wish I could make you see."

He regarded her so steadily. "I think I do see. I don't like it. I think you're punishing yourself for something that really isn't your fault. But I get it. I do." He looked so exhausted, suddenly.

And seriously, who would have guessed that sexy, charming, commitment-phobic Liam Bravo would grow up to be such an amazing man?

She reached out a tentative hand and combed his hair

back with her fingers. He didn't duck away. She tried to take heart from that. "You look worn-out—worn-out from dealing with me."

He caught her hand, opened her fingers and kissed the center of her palm. His lips were so warm, his breath a caress in itself. "Let's try to get some sleep, okay?"

"Yeah. Okay."

They settled down into the bed. He turned off the light and then pulled her in close. She cuddled against him, grateful for his arms around her.

And all too aware that she was the one holding them back.

Karin opened her eyes to daylight.

Morning?

It was morning already? She slid her hand across the bottom sheet.

Empty.

Liam had left the bed.

"No!" She popped straight up to a sitting position, her heart going a mile a minute.

The kids would already be up by now. Up and wondering where Mom had gotten off to.

And her dad...

She'd never asked him outright to keep her nighttime visits with Liam a secret. What if he took her staying here till morning as a signal that she and Liam were outing their relationship? What if he just told her son and her daughter that she was over here? What if he sent Coco to summon them to breakfast?

Uh-uh. No way. The kids were not supposed to know about her and Liam. They weren't supposed to get their hopes up, to start counting on him to be there, be a real father to them, as the years went by.

Because no matter how sure Liam seemed now—getting down on one knee, whipping out the most beautiful ring she'd ever seen, telling her he loved her and asking her to marry him...

He could so easily change his mind, move back to his big house in Astoria, come by Sweetheart Cove only to pick up and drop off his son.

Coco and Ben would be devastated.

No. That couldn't happen. Her kids were innocent. They didn't deserve that kind of pain. They'd already suffered enough in their short lives.

"Liam...?" She heard water running.

The door to the master bath stood open.

The shower.

He was taking a shower.

How could he have just left the bed without waking her up? How could he be so thoughtless?

He knew she should have been back at the other house long before now.

Furious, literally shaking with frustration, she jumped from the bed and started grabbing her wrinkled clothes, yanking them on as fast as she got hold of them.

The water shut off. By then, she'd dropped to the bed again to put on her ankle boots. Liam emerged from the bathroom, a towel around his lean hips, a tender smile on his lips. He looked so manly, lean and tall, like every woman's perfect fantasy man, his hard biceps flexing as he rubbed his wet hair with a second towel.

And for some reason, his tender smile, that easy way about him, it all just made her madder than ever.

She tugged on the second boot and jumped up to face him. "What is the matter with you?"

He stopped drying his hair. Endless seconds elapsed

before he said quietly, "Nothing. Nothing's the matter with me."

"Why didn't you wake me?"

He tossed the towel on a chair. "You looked tired, so I let you sleep."

She wanted to start shrieking at him, to grab him and shake him until he realized how careless he'd been. "You knew I needed to get back. The kids will be up now. What am I going to say to them?"

"Karin. You don't have to *say* anything to them. They won't be damaged for life just because you spent the night over here." He spoke to her so gently, carefully, like she was a crazy person throwing a fit.

And maybe she kind of was. Somewhere in the back of her mind she knew she was behaving very badly. "You are so irresponsible," she accused, though he wasn't. He was wonderful, always there when she needed him, always patient and thoughtful and ready to help.

She was totally overreacting, her heart aching from his beautiful proposal she couldn't allow herself to accept. She knew, absolutely, that one way or another, she was going to lose him. She just didn't know when it was going to happen.

She wished he would just get it over with and leave her, already.

"Liam, I can't do this. I'm so sorry, but we have to stop this. I want you to please go see your lawyer. I want you to decide what kind of parenting plan works for you. Then we can come to an agreement on custody and all that. We need to move on. We need to settle this once and for all."

He just stood there in his towel, looking handsome and bleak, staring at her.

* * *

For Liam, it happened right then, as they stared at each other across a distance of maybe ten feet that suddenly yawned wide as the Grand Canyon. He realized he'd reached his breaking point with her.

He couldn't take anymore. It just wasn't going to work with her. He'd knocked himself out trying to show her how much he loved her and wanted a life with her. But she just would not believe him.

At some point, a guy had to salvage the last of his pride, take the diamond ring back to Tiffany & Co. and get on with his own damn life.

"Fair enough," he said, his own voice dead, flat in his ears. "I'll talk to my lawyer."

She had the nerve to look stricken. Like *he'd* just hurt *her.* "Good," she said, the word breaking a little in the middle. "Talk to your lawyer—and you'll move back to your own house?"

That, he wouldn't do. "I want time with my son and living here is the best way for me to get that. And truthfully, I promised Ben I wouldn't leave. I'm living in this cottage for as long as Sten is willing to keep cashing my checks. If you don't want to be with me, well, that's up to you. But I live here now, Karin. And I'm not going anywhere."

Chapter Thirteen

Karin walked out.

She grabbed her coat from the peg by the front door and went back to the other house. What else could she do? She'd pretty much wrecked everything. Better to just get the hell out.

At the main house, they were all gathered around the breakfast table—the kids, her dad, Sten and Madison. She walked in and they all turned and looked at her.

"Where's Liam?" Ben asked.

She waved a hand, trying to look casual and easy and probably blowing that all to hell. "Oh, he'll be over in a minute, I'm sure." Her gaze collided with Sten's and she *knew* that *he* knew something was terribly wrong. She blinked and looked away—but not far enough to escape the concerned frown on her dad's face.

Right then, the baby monitor on the counter erupted with fussy cries. She had never in her life felt so relieved to hear her baby crying. "I'll, um, just go take care of him…" And she fled for the sanctuary of Riley's room.

After she'd fed and changed the baby and pulled herself together a little, Karin returned to the kitchen. The adults had dispersed, which suited her just fine. Coco and Ben were clearing off the table.

"There's eggs and bacon left for you," said Ben.

"Great. Thanks." She put Riley in his bouncy seat and sat down to eat in spite of the fact that she had zero appetite.

Coco stepped close. She wrapped her arms around Karin's neck, rested her head on Karin's shoulder and said wistfully, "I love you, Mommy."

Kids. They always sensed when things were off with the grown-ups. Karin patted the small hands clasped around her neck. "Love you, too. So much."

Coco pulled away, but then took the seat next to Karin's. "Sten and Madison and Dirk and Sergei are taking us to the ranch where Aislinn lives today." Aislinn was the Bravo sister born to Lloyd and Paula Delaney, the one who'd been switched with Madison the day they were born. Madison was slowly getting to know all her newfound brothers and sisters, but she and Aislinn had hit it off from the first. The two shared a special bond. "We're going to have lunch there," Coco added. "Madison says Aislinn has rabbits that live on her porch and we get to pet them."

"That's great." Karin sincerely hoped she sounded at least a little enthusiastic.

"Liam never came," Ben said too quietly from over by the sink.

Karin turned in her chair to meet her son's serious eyes. "I'm sure he'll be over later." Truthfully, she kind of wished that Liam wouldn't be over at all, though it was both wrong and ridiculous for her to wish such a thing. His son lived here. He was friends with her father. He had actual relationships with her older children.

He'd said it repeatedly himself. He was not going anywhere.

Well, except for as far away from her as he could get. She'd made sure of that.

Liam spent most of the day at the Warrenton terminal. Around five when he packed it in, he was tempted to take a little detour on the way home to the cottage. There were bars on Beach Street calling his name.

But he intended to be at Karin's for breakfast the next morning, whether she wanted him there or not. No way he was showing up at her table with a hangover.

Uh-uh. He needed a clear head tomorrow. He would see the kids and reach an understanding with their mother that nothing had changed in terms of RG. He would have his son from nine to noon Wednesdays and Fridays, as per their prior agreement. And she would damn well reach out to him if she needed someone to watch the baby any other time.

At the cottage, he had a beer and nuked himself some frozen lasagna. Once he'd shoved down the food, he considered calling Deke Pasternak and making an appointment to talk about custody and a damn parenting plan. He'd told Karin he would.

But later for that. Right now, RG needed him nearby and available. He was both. Problem solved.

Just as he began considering the big question of whether or not to have a second beer, he heard footsteps out on the deck. For about a half a second, his heart bounced toward his throat and hope exploded in his chest.

But it wasn't Karin.

It was Ben, sweet, serious Ben. The kid looked apprehensive and that had Liam pissed off at Karin all over again.

He got up and pushed open the slider. "Come on in."

The wind was blowing, the sky thick with dark clouds, the waves out beyond the beach tossing and foaming. Ben hunched into his down jacket, like a turtle seeking the safety of his shell. "I can't stay very long."

Liam stepped out of the way. "Get in here. It's cold out there." The boy crossed the threshold and Liam shut the glass door. "Want some hot chocolate or something?"

"No, thanks." Ben shoved his hands even deeper into his jacket pockets. "So. You and Mom are fighting?"

Liam saw it all in those serious brown eyes. Ben had lost his father. Now he anticipated losing Liam, too—and right now, the boy was waiting for Liam to say something, to somehow ease his fears. Too bad Liam had nothing all that encouraging to say. "Your mom and I are having some problems, yes."

"What problems?"

"Ben, I can't go into detail about it, but things aren't good between your mom and me right now."

Ben's face started to crumple—but he kept it together, straightening his narrow shoulders, hiking up his chin. "So, you're moving out?"

That, he could answer more emphatically. "Nope. I'll be here. I live here."

"What about breakfast tomorrow?"

"I'll be there."

"Yeah?"

"You have my word on it."

"What about Christmas? You still cooking breakfast for us Christmas morning?"

"That is my plan." If Karin thought differently, well, they would have to discuss it. She would actually have to *talk* to him. That could be good, right?

Or maybe not.

Ben wasn't finished. "And will you be there Christmas Eve and are we all going up to the Bravo house for Christmas dinner?"

In spite of how craptacular he felt at that moment, Liam almost smiled. "How come you didn't ask your mom all these questions?"

Ben gulped. "I kind of had a feeling I would get better answers from you."

Liam wanted to grab the kid and hug him, but he had a suspicion that any sudden moves on his part wouldn't be welcome right now. Ben needed reassurance that the ground was solid under his feet, that the people he'd come to count on and trust wouldn't abandon him, no matter what weird stuff happened between the grown-ups. "I'm not sure about all our specific plans. What I am sure about is that I'm going to be here, just like I said I would. No matter what happens, that's not going to change."

"Not ever?"

"Not for a long while, anyway. You've got my number." Ben had his own phone. They'd exchanged numbers back in October, the first time Liam drove him to soccer practice. "Anytime you need to talk to me, you just call, text or show up at my door."

Ben yanked his right hand from his pocket and stuck it out. Liam shook it.

The hug happened after all when Ben kind of swayed toward him and Liam put his free arm around him.

Ben quickly stepped back. "Okay, then. I just needed to know. See you for breakfast." He turned and shoved the slider wide, stepped through and closed it. With a last, solemn nod at Liam through the glass, he took off across the deck.

"What's going on with you and Liam?" Otto asked Karin that night when the kids were in bed and Sten and Madison had gone upstairs.

"I don't want to talk about it, Dad. I really don't."

"That man's in love with you. And you're in love with him. Whatever it is, you need to work it out with him."

"Stay out of it, Dad."

He narrowed his eyes at her and put on his stern voice. "Fix it."

She knew with absolute certainty that she was about to burst into tears. "Please, Dad…"

His hard expression melted as he reached out his big hands and clasped her shoulders. "Aw, honey."

She sagged against him and whispered, "I messed up. I messed up bad."

He patted her back. "Now, now. You'll work it out, I know you will."

"I don't think so, Dad. I was terrible to him. He's not going to forgive me and I can't say I blame him."

"Love forgives all. Just give it time…"

An hour later, when she couldn't sleep, she put on thermal pants and a heavy sweater, her shearling boots, a winter jacket, mittens and a beanie, grabbed Riley's monitor and went out to sit on the deck. She wasn't the least surprised when Sten, as bundled up as she was, came out the door behind her and took the empty chair at her side.

All the wise advice she'd given him back in April

when he screwed things up with Madison seemed to hover in the cold night air between them, taunting her.

"Colder than a polar bear's nose," he said mildly. "At least the wind's died down a little."

She wrapped her arms a little tighter around herself. "Don't start in on me, Sten. Please?"

He gave a wry chuckle. "Talk of the weather really bugs the crap out of you, huh?"

She huffed out a breath. "Okay, fine. Just say it."

"Not sure where to start. I don't know what's wrong between you and Liam, not really."

She tugged her beanie more firmly down over her ears. "I jumped all over him for no reason at all."

"Oh, come on. There had to be a reason."

"Yeah, well, not an *acceptable* reason. He asked me to marry him and that scared me to death—and let me be clear. I did worse than jump all over him. I told him we were done and he should move back to Astoria and come up with a parenting plan."

He made a thoughtful sound. "You're in love with the guy, right?"

She stared out at the restless gray ocean beyond the wide stretch of sand and found it surprisingly easy to tell her brother the truth. "I am, yeah. I am very much in love with Liam Bravo."

"I used to think you would never marry anyone again, that Bud was your true, forever love, lost tragically at sea, but you'd learned to be happy with the kids, on your own."

She groaned. "So romantic."

"Yeah, well. I never did want to think there might be big issues between you and Bud."

"There were. I never should have married him. He

wasn't ready. I wasn't ready. The love we had was…
not that strong."

"This love you have with Liam, is it *that* strong?"

She didn't even have to think about it. "Yeah—but
what if I'm wrong? So far, I've kept him at a distance
by making him promise that what we have would stay
just between the two of us. When he asked me to marry
him last night, I turned him down. Then I drummed up
a fake reason to break it off between us. I love my children, and you and Dad. But my track record at loving
a man? We should face it. It's not good."

"Someone very wise once told me that I shouldn't let
getting my heart broken by the wrong person keep me
from giving the right person a fighting chance. Take
your own advice. Give the *right* man a chance."

"How did I know you were going to say that?"

He grinned. "Super painful, isn't it? When your own
words come back to bite you in the ass…"

The next morning, Liam showed up for breakfast.
Coco ran and hugged him. Everyone else played it cool
and subdued.

Karin ached all over just to see him sitting there at
the table with Riley asleep in a sling strapped to the
front of him.

So close.

But no longer *hers*.

The plans for Christmas Eve and Christmas Day
were brought up and reconfirmed. Karin didn't make a
peep when that happened. Liam didn't have to be hers
to be part of the family. He was Madison's brother and
Riley's dad. And even if he wasn't *hers*, Coco and Ben
had definitely come to think of him as *theirs*.

When he got up to go, he still had Riley hooked to

the front of him. "So, Karin, how about if I just take RG with me now? You can pick him up at noon, or whatever. Just take your time."

"Um, that would be great." She smiled at him. It was more of a grimace, really. But hey, at least she tried. She filled an insulated pack with bottles of breast milk to replenish the stash at his place and sent him on his way.

And then, somehow, she got through her morning and showed up at Liam's door at noon on the nose. He had Riley all ready to go. The handoff took maybe a minute. She tried not to look directly at Liam. She had this feeling that if she actually met his eyes, she would drop to her knees and start pleading with him to give her one more chance.

In a way, dropping to her knees kind of seemed like a viable approach to this huge problem she'd created. But she was so afraid he'd turn her down, that he'd realized he'd been all wrong to want to build a life with her. He would say no.

And she would have to know for certain it was over. She just couldn't face that. Not yet.

Liam planned to go up to the Warrenton terminal as soon as Karin came for RG. But the sight of her just kind of broke him. She was trying so hard to be civil, even kind. He'd expected her to give him dirty looks when he showed up for breakfast, to put up a fight about what to do for Christmas, to insist that really, the plans they'd made earlier needed to change.

Those things didn't happen. She nodded when the rest of them agreed that the Christmas schedule would stay the same. And then, at noon, when she came to pick up RG, he'd been sure she would start in about the damn parenting plan.

Nope. She thanked him, forced a smile, took the baby and left.

If she'd only been a jerk to him, he would have found it at least a little easier to hold on to his anger with her. Instead, he missed her, *ached* for her, wished he could find a way to heal the breach between them.

Not thirty-six hours after he'd lost her, he was already trying to figure out how to find his way back to her.

Yesterday, he'd had some vague idea that he'd head down to Portland today after Karin came for RG, that he would check in at his offices there and take the ring back to Tiffany & Co.

But now he realized that what he really needed was someone he could trust to talk to.

He thought of Otto first. He really did trust Karin's dad and the man was older, much wiser and good at heart, with that understanding way about him.

But Otto was Karin's dad. And dragging Otto into this, putting him in a position where he might feel he had to take sides...

Uh-uh. That wouldn't be right.

Liam called Daniel. It turned out his oldest brother was spending the day before Christmas Eve at home with his family.

At a little after one, Liam was sitting on the sofa in Daniel's study at the house on Rinehart Hill.

"Scotch?" asked his older brother as he poured two fingers for himself. Daniel inevitably brought out the good Scotch for man-to-man talks.

"Thanks, but no."

"So, what's going on?" Daniel carried his drink over to the chair across from Liam.

And Liam laid it on him. "I'm in love with Karin—

completely. It's deep, Daniel, what I feel for her. And it's real. I bought a ring and then night-before-last I asked her to marry me. She said she loves me, too, but she put the brakes on, turned me down." He recounted in detail the story of the fight and the breakup that had occurred early yesterday morning.

When he finally fell silent, Daniel said, "And then you realized you were wrong and you don't love her after all?"

Suddenly, Liam wished he'd taken that drink. "What the hell, Daniel? No. Uh-uh. I do love her. She's everything to me."

Daniel sipped his Scotch. "You still want to marry her, then?"

"You bet your ass I do. I just, well, what did I do wrong and how can I make it right?"

"Judging by what you've just told me, you didn't do anything wrong."

"I didn't…? Daniel, if I didn't do anything wrong, then there is no way for me to make it right."

"Not by yourself. At some point, she's going to need to meet you halfway."

"I don't know. It's really hard for her. She had a bad experience with Bud Killigan."

"Not your fault. But you said that *she* said she loves you, right?"

"She did, yeah."

"So stay steady. Don't let her fear scare you away."

Easier said than done. "You know how I am. I get enthusiastic. And that makes me impatient. I *knew* I should've waited. I *planned* to wait until she was more sure of me, of *us*. But then she said she loved me and I completely lost my head. I grabbed the ring and got down on my knees."

"That's okay. You got a right to be you, man."

"I just don't know how you do it, Daniel. How you've done it for all these years, the way you've put up with all of us, *been there* for all of us, even with all the crap we've laid on you, all the challenges we've thrown at you."

Daniel gave a slow, pensive shake of his head. "I've made some giant mistakes along the way."

"Maybe, but you hung in. You always found a way to make it right. No matter how bad things got, you kept stepping up."

Daniel set down his drink and leaned forward in his chair. "And that—what you just said. That's how you do it. That's how you make it work. You have to be there when you're needed—you have to be there just *in case* you're needed. And don't even try to kid yourself, you will always wonder if you're doing it right, if you're messing something up that's going to make it harder for someone you love down the line. No matter what, though, you do the best you can. And sometimes you screw it up. And then you scramble to try to make it right again. But you can never get it right if you don't keep putting yourself out there in the first place."

Bolstered by his big brother's advice, Liam decided that he would reach out to Karin again.

This time though, he would be reasonable and careful. He would make it crystal clear to her that he didn't want to push her, he just wanted to be with her—yeah, he wanted to marry her. He wanted her for today and tomorrow and the rest of their lives.

But if one day at a time was the only way she could do it, one day at a time was just fine with him.

And if she still needed to keep what they had together a secret from Ben and Coco, he would respect her wishes and make certain she got back to the main house every morning before dawn.

At first, he was thinking he couldn't wait. That he needed to try to make things right with her immediately.

But that was just his impatient nature taking over again.

He ordered himself to slow down, to think it through more carefully. It was the day before Christmas Eve. He didn't want to mess up the fragile peace between them. Coco and Ben were counting on their Christmas plans. He couldn't take the chance that Karin would not only turn him down, but decide she just wasn't comfortable having breakfast at the cottage Christmas morning or going to Daniel's for Christmas Day.

No. He needed to wait at least until the day after Christmas to try to make things right with her.

Instead of heading back to the Cove and pounding on her door or blowing up her phone with calls and texts, he went into downtown Valentine Bay.

He loved his hometown at Christmas. All the shop windows had Christmas displays and the streetlamps were wrapped in garland and hung with lighted wreathes. He dropped some bills into a couple of Salvation Army pots and did some last-minute Christmas shopping, more gifts for Ben and Coco, Otto and Sten and his nieces and nephew.

At some point, he started thinking about all the families who couldn't afford piles of presents under their trees. So he bought even more toys and made a quick run by Safeway and Walgreens to help fill the Toys for Tots donation boxes. Before he went home, he stopped at a diner he liked for a quick dinner.

Back at the cottage by seven, he turned on the Christmas lights inside and out, cued up the holiday tunes and spent a couple of hours wrapping the gifts he'd found on his impromptu shopping spree.

It was snowing at nine fifteen when he stuck a bow on the last package and got up to put it under the tree. He heard footsteps on the deck and glanced up to see Karin standing on the far side of the sliding door.

For a moment, he almost didn't believe his own eyes.

But then she raised a hand and gave him a sheepish wave.

Real. She was real.

His blood racing through his veins and his breath all tangled and hot in his chest, he went to let her in.

Chapter Fourteen

Snowflakes glittered in her hair and her cheeks were pink from the cold. She gave him a beautiful, wobbly little smile. "Dad's got Riley. I was hoping we could talk." The look in her eyes? It promised him everything.

He wanted to grab her, wrap her up tight in his arms and never, ever let go.

But then he reminded himself that she'd only said she wanted to talk. The thing *not* to do right now was make wild assumptions.

"Yes," he said. "I would love to talk."

"So then, may I come in?"

Feeling foolish for keeping her standing out in the cold, he stepped clear of the doorway. "Please."

She entered the kitchen and he shut and locked the slider.

"Here. Give me your coat." He moved behind her.

She let him slip it off her shoulders. He laid it over the back of a kitchen chair. "Tea? Hot chocolate?"

"No. I just want to talk."

He ushered her over to the fire. They sat on the hearth side by side.

"You're busy," she said nervously, gesturing at the coffee table, where he'd left the rolls of bright wrapping paper and the big bag of ready-made bows.

"Nope. I'm all done." He turned and stared directly at her then—like a gift in itself, just looking at her. "I have wrapped the last present." And damn it, he couldn't wait another second to touch her. He reached for her hand.

And she gave it, her slim fingers sliding between his, weaving them together.

It was everything he'd ever wanted, her hand in his. He was so glad he'd waited, given her time to come back to him when she was ready—and was he jumping the gun again? Assuming more than she was offering?

"Talk to me," he said.

Her eyes were dark with shadows. "If I talk about the past...is that okay?"

"Anything, Karin. Everything. I want to understand. I want to be the one you come to—for the good things. And for the tough things, too."

"I, um…" She hesitated. He made himself be quiet, made himself simply wait as she blew out a slow breath and tried again. "I didn't love Bud—I mean, I didn't love him enough. Not the way a woman needs to love a man she builds a life with. I married him because he said he loved *me*, because I was pregnant and worried about the future. Saying yes to him seemed like the answer to a bunch of questions I didn't even really know how to ask. It was not the best choice. It was, in the end, a pretty bad choice, to marry Bud. And when he died, I swear I felt like I had killed him."

He couldn't let that stand. "No. What happened to him wasn't your fault."

She leaned her head on his shoulder. "You're right. I know that I didn't *really* kill him. But for a long time, I blamed myself for his death."

"But not anymore?"

"No. Bud really was like those songs you hear and those books you read about sailors. He was married to the sea. He loved the life on a fishing boat. And he died doing what he loved. I can't say I take comfort from that, exactly, but it is what it is and at least I'm no longer telling myself it was all my fault. I've made a lot of progress with that."

He kind of wanted to scold her for ever having blamed herself. But this was *her* story she was sharing. He had no right to tell her how to feel about her part in it.

She lifted her head from his shoulder and grinned at him. "Look at you. So restrained."

"I'm trying." He pressed their joined hands to his heart. "Go on."

She drew in a slow breath. "So, I got over blaming myself for Bud's death. However, I have remained absolutely determined never to make the same mistake I made with Bud. I have sworn to myself that I will never again marry a man for the wrong reason." She gazed directly into his eyes. "But what is the wrong reason? *That's* what I didn't really understand—not until the last couple of days. Not until I felt I had lost you. Only since then have I started to see that the wrong reason wasn't about the baby I was going to have. It had nothing to do with being pregnant. It was about the love. I didn't love Bud enough. And for that reason and that reason alone, I had no right to marry him." Her eyes gleamed so bright. A tear escaped and slid down her cheek.

"Don't cry, sweetheart." Liam leaned in and kissed the wetness away. "I love you. I want you. I want a life with you. I love you way more than enough."

She touched his cheek with her free hand, a quick brush of a touch, too quickly gone. "When I put off telling you I was having your baby, it was because I knew you were a stand-up guy, and I was dreading that you might ask me to marry you for the same reason Bud had, because you felt obligated."

His laugh sounded pained to his own ears. "Okay, yeah. In the beginning, that day I spotted you at Safeway and the truth came out, I honestly didn't know my ass from up. I was only trying really hard to do the right thing."

She sniffled a little, smiling at him through her tears. "And I knew that."

"But doing the right thing isn't the reason I want to marry you now. Not anymore. Everything's changed now. Now I've figured out what I had no damn clue about for way too long. Not back in high school. Not last winter, in those amazing nights you gave me before you broke it off. And not that day in October when I finally found out I was going to be a dad."

She searched his face. "What? Tell me."

"I've figured out why I could never really get you out of my mind. I understand now why I was pissed off when I heard you'd married Bud, why, through all the years since high school, I've always felt this pinch in my chest whenever I thought of you. It's because you're the one. The one for me. I do love you, Karin. I will always love you. More than I'm ever going to know how to say."

Karin just stared at him.

He squeezed her hand. "What did I do?"

"Liam, you said exactly what I needed to hear."

"But are you okay?"

She drew a slow, shaky breath. "Never better. And I mean that sincerely."

Holding hands was not enough. He pulled her into his arms. She lifted her beautiful face to him.

And he kissed her, deep and slow and infinitely sweet.

"I love you, Liam Bravo," she said when he lifted his head. "So much. Way more than enough to last through the hard times. I love you enough to be with you forever."

"So then, it's good that I didn't take the ring back?"

"Yes." She kissed him again, hard and quick. "Yes, to everything. To that amazing, perfect ring you chose for me. To the future. To our wedding. To me staying right here with you all night long and then the two of us going to the other house together for breakfast tomorrow, where we will break the big news to the family that we're getting married."

Maybe his mouth was hanging open. A little. "You mean that?"

"I do. Every word."

He pressed his lips to the velvety skin at her temple. "Well, all right then. Count me in." He claimed her mouth again, a kiss that melted into another kiss and another after that.

A while later, they turned off the fire and switched off the lights. He led her down the hall to his room.

"I should probably be patient," he said, "but I'm going for it anyway. I don't want to wait. I want to get married right away. If that doesn't work for you, just say so right now."

"Yes."

He blinked down at her. "Yes, you agree to getting married right away?"

Her grin was slow and full of equal parts joy and mischief. "Maybe at New Year's?"

He couldn't stop himself. He pushed his luck some more. "Matt and Sabra got married last New Year's. It was just the family and close friends, at Daniel's house."

She didn't balk, didn't even ask for time to think it over. "I would love that."

It was stacking up to be the best Christmas ever. "We can discuss the idea with Keely and Daniel on Christmas Day."

"Totally works for me."

Had he ever been this happy? He couldn't remember when. "Wait right here?"

"Yes."

He was back with her in under thirty seconds. She gave him her hand and he slipped on the ring he'd chosen for her. It fit perfectly. The saleswoman at Tiffany & Co. had helped him guesstimate the size.

"I love it," she said and reached up to frame his face in her two soft hands. "I love *you*."

"I love you, Karin Killigan. And I will be loving you every single day for the rest of our lives."

"We did it all backward," she whispered. "This shouldn't be possible. But somehow, it's all come out absolutely right."

They were married on New Year's Day at the house on Rhinehart Hill. A trucker friend of Liam's who also happened to be an ordained minister officiated. Karin had no bridesmaids and Liam skipped the groomsmen.

The bride and groom stood up together in a room full of family and friends, with Ben on Liam's side and Coco next to Karin. Riley George slept through the brief ceremony, held close in his father's loving arms.

They settled in together at the main house on Sweetheart Cove. Sten sold Liam the cottage for a bargain price and Liam had the cottage rebuilt to accommodate a growing family. By the time Sten and a very pregnant Madison returned to Valentine Bay to make their home in the main house, the cottage was ready for Liam, Karin, the kids and Otto.

A year later, Karin gave birth to another boy. They named him Aiden at Coco's request.

* * * * *

*Watch for Grace Bravo's story,
coming in May 2020,
only from Harlequin Special Edition.*

*And be sure to catch up on the rest of
The Bravos of Valentine Bay miniseries
with these great romances by Christine Rimmer:*

A Husband She Couldn't Forget
Switched at Birth
Same Time, Next Christmas
Almost a Bravo
The Nanny's Double Trouble

*Available now wherever Harlequin Special Edition
books and ebooks are sold!*

WE HOPE YOU ENJOYED THIS BOOK!

HARLEQUIN®

SPECIAL EDITION

Open your heart to more true-to-life stories of love and family.

Discover six new books available every month, wherever books are sold.

HSEHALO0419

THE RIGHT REASON TO MARRY
The Bravos of Valentine Bay • by Christine Rimmer

Unexpected fatherhood changes everything for charming bachelor Liam Bravo. He wants to marry Karin Killigan, the mother of his child. But Karin won't settle for less than lasting true love.

MAVERICK CHRISTMAS SURPRISE
Montana Mavericks: Six Brides for Six Brothers
by Brenda Harlen

Rancher Wilder Crawford is in no hurry to get married and start a family—until a four-month-old baby is left on his doorstep on Christmas Day!

THE RANCHER'S BEST GIFT
Men of the West • by Stella Bagwell

Rancher Matthew Waggoner was planning to be in and out of Red Bluff as quickly as possible. But staying with his boss's sister, Camille Hollister, proves to be more enticing than he thought. Will these two opposites be able to work through their differences and get the best Christmas gift?

IT STARTED AT CHRISTMAS...
Gallant Lake Stories • by Jo McNally

Despite lying on her résumé, Amanda Lowery still manages to land a job designing Halcyon House for Blake Randall—and a place to stay over Christmas. Neither of them have had much to celebrate, but with Blake's grieving nephew staying at Halcyon, they're all hoping for some Christmas magic.

A TALE OF TWO CHRISTMAS LETTERS
Texas Legends: The McCabes • by Cathy Gillen Thacker

Rehab nurse Bess Monroe is mortified that she accidentally sent out two Christmas letters—one telling the world about her lonely life instead of the positive spin she wanted! And when Jack McCabe, widowed surgeon and father of three, sees the second one, he offers his friendship to get through the holidays. But their pact soon turns into something more...

THE SOLDIER'S SECRET SON
The Culhanes of Cedar River • by Helen Lacey

When Jake Culhane comes home to Cedar River, he doesn't expect to reconnect with the woman he never forgot. Abby Perkins is still in love with the boy who broke her heart when he enlisted. This could be their first Christmas as a real family—if Abby can find the courage to tell Jake the truth.

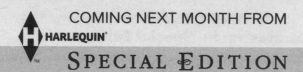
Available December 17, 2019

#2737 FORTUNE'S FRESH START
The Fortunes of Texas: Rambling Rose • by Michelle Major
In the small Texas burg of Rambling Rose, real estate investor Callum Fortune is making a big splash. The last thing he needs is any personal complications slowing his pace—least of all nurse Becky Averill, a beautiful widow with twin baby girls!

#2738 HER RIGHT-HAND COWBOY
Forever, Texas • by Marie Ferrarella
A clause in her father's will requires Ena O'Rourke to work the family ranch for six months before she can sell it. She's livid at her father throwing a wrench in her life from beyond the grave. But Mitch Randall, foreman of the Double E, is always there for her. As Ena spends more time on the ranch—and with Mitch—new memories are laid over the old...and perhaps new opportunities to make a life.

#2739 SECOND-CHANCE SWEET SHOP
Wickham Falls Weddings • by Rochelle Alers
Brand-new bakery owner Sasha Manning didn't anticipate that the teenager she hired would have a father more delectable than anything in her shop window! Sasha still smarts from falling for a man too good to be true. Divorced single dad Dwight Adams will have to prove to Sasha that he's the real deal and not a wolf in sheep's clothing...and learn to trust someone with his heart along the way.

#2740 COOKING UP ROMANCE
The Taylor Triplets • by Lynne Marshall
Lacy was a redhead with a pink food truck who prepared mouthwatering meals. Hunky construction manager Zack Gardner agreed to let her feed his hungry crew in exchange for cooking lessons for his young daughter. But it looked like the lovely businesswoman was transforming the single dad's life in more ways than one—since a family secret is going to change both of their lives in ways they never expected.

#2741 RELUCTANT HOMETOWN HERO
Wildfire Ridge • by Heatherly Bell
Former army officer Ryan Davis doesn't relish the high-profile role of town sheriff, but when duty calls, he responds. Even if it means helping animal rescuer Zoey Castillo find her missing foster dog. When Ryan asks her out, Zoey is wary of a relationship in the spotlight—especially given her past. If the sheriff wants to date her, he'll have to prove that two legs are better than four.

#2742 THE WEDDING TRUCE
Something True • by Kerri Carpenter
For the sake of their best friends' wedding, divorce attorney Xander Ryan and wedding planner Grace Harris are calling a truce. Now they must plan the perfect wedding shower together. But Xander doesn't believe in marriage! And Grace believes in romance and true love. Clearly, they have nothing in common. In fact, all Xander feels when Grace is near is disdain and...desire. Wait. What?

YOU CAN FIND MORE INFORMATION ON UPCOMING HARLEQUIN® TITLES, FREE EXCERPTS AND MORE AT WWW.HARLEQUIN.COM.

HSECNM1219

SPECIAL EXCERPT FROM

H HARLEQUIN®

SPECIAL EDITION

In the small Texas burg of Rambling Rose, real estate
investor Callum Fortune is making a big splash.
The last thing he needs is any personal complications
slowing his pace—least of all nurse Becky Averill,
a beautiful widow with twin baby girls!

Read on for a sneak preview of
Fortune's Fresh Start
by Michelle Major, the first book in
The Fortunes of Texas: Rambling Rose continuity.

"I didn't mean to rush off the other day after the ribbon cutting," he told her as they approached the door that led to the childcare center. "I think I interrupted a potential invitation for dinner, and I've been regretting it ever since."

Becky blinked. In truth, she would have never had the guts to invite Callum for dinner. She'd been planning to offer to cook or bake for him and drop it off at his office as a thank-you. The idea of having him over to her small house did funny things to her insides.

"Oh," she said again.

"Maybe I misinterpreted," Callum said quickly, looking as flummoxed as she felt. "Or imagined the whole thing. You meant to thank me with a bottle of wine or some cookies or—"

"Dinner." She grinned at him. Somehow his discomposure gave her the confidence to say the word.

He appeared so perfect and out of her league, but at the moment he simply seemed like a normal, nervous guy not sure what to say next.

She decided to make it easy for him. For both of them. "Would you come for dinner tomorrow night? The girls go to bed early, so if you could be there around seven, we could have a more leisurely meal and a chance to talk."

His shoulders visibly relaxed. "I'd like that. Dinner with a friend. Can I bring anything?"

"Just yourself," she told him.

He pulled his cell phone from his pocket and handed it to her so she could enter her contact information. It took a few tries to get it right because her fingers trembled slightly.

He grinned at her as he took the phone again. "I'm looking forward to tomorrow, Becky."

"Me, too," she breathed, then gave a little wave as he said goodbye. She took a few steadying breaths before heading in to pick up the twins. *Don't turn it into something more than it is*, she cautioned herself.

It was a thank-you, not a date. Her babies would be asleep in the next room. Definitely not a date.

But her stammering heart didn't seem to get the message.

Don't miss
Fortune's Fresh Start *by Michelle Major,*
available January 2020 wherever
Harlequin® *Special Edition books and ebooks are sold.*

Harlequin.com

Love Harlequin romance?

DISCOVER.

Be the first to find out about promotions, news and exclusive content!

f Facebook.com/HarlequinBooks

t Twitter.com/HarlequinBooks

○ Instagram.com/HarlequinBooks

p Pinterest.com/HarlequinBooks

ReaderService.com

EXPLORE.

Sign up for the Harlequin e-newsletter and download a free book from any series at **TryHarlequin.com.**

CONNECT.

Join our Harlequin community to share your thoughts and connect with other romance readers!
Facebook.com/groups/HarlequinConnection

HARLEQUIN®

**ROMANCE WHEN
YOU NEED IT**

HSOCIAL2018